THE GENTLE
BOMBER'S MELODY

Edward D. Webster

ISBN 10: 0615894534
ISBN 13: 9780615894539
Library of Congress Control Number: 2013953438
Dream House Press, Ojai, CA

To John R. Webster
Historical novelist
Big brother
Friend

Acknowledgements

I wish to thank retired FBI Special Agent James Motz for his assistance with technical details and Steve Efner for computer/Internet-related guidance. I also appreciate Vivian Sudhalter's editing skill and helpful ideas and my writers' group for their excellent forthright criticism.

And thank you, Marguerite, my dear one. Your support and suggestions, as always, have been terrific.

Disclaimer

This book is fiction, invented by the author and not intended to depict any real person or event.

Chapter 1

Melody spotted a sign for Cimarron and veered left onto New Mexico 58. Now that she was off the interstate; there'd be fewer cop patrols. She goosed the accelerator and glanced in the rearview—no one following.

If only she could shake this crazy jittery feeling. *The police can't be after me*, she thought. *At least not yet.*

Melody knew from TV crime shows—if they had cameras in the halls of the hospital back in Santa Fe, they'd have her picture. But the wig and fake glasses would throw them. As she'd carried the baby to the stairwell, she'd looked down, away from any cameras. And she lived in another state; no one in New Mexico knew her. Still, her hand shook every time she took it off the steering wheel.

She wanted to look at the baby in the back seat, but she kept her eyes on the curving road.

She had messed up in one area, she knew, but Melody didn't want to think about it. What had her shrink said years ago? *You ignore obvious problems to make the future look rosy.* Well the future *would* be rosy now, damn it.

"Hi, little Heather," she called.

The shrink had demanded that she face her mistakes. OK. What she'd forgotten were the security cameras that could be recording the hospital parking lot.

The road straightened, and she turned to glance back at Heather asleep in the baby seat. Heather hadn't been the name on the infant's bassinet at the hospital. But it was her name now.

"It's gonna be OK, sweetie," she said to Heather.

She turned on the radio and spun the dial until she found an Oldies station. The words blared out, *All alone am I, ever since your goodbye.* Tears trickled from Melody's eyes. "I've been alone my whole life," she said to the baby. "But not any more. Now I got you, Heather."

Reduced speed ahead. Melody slowed to 35, passing a sign that said "Cimarron, N.M. population 816." The wig and glasses now lay on the passenger seat, and she felt conspicuous in the yellow nurse's smock. There was nothing much along the highway—just a few mobile homes and industrial buildings—so she turned the old Escort down a side street into town. She spotted a run-down building, dirty white stucco with a wide wooden porch and a sign: Cimarron General Store. An old store like that wouldn't have surveillance cameras.

She swung around back of the store, halting by the dinged-up blue dumpster. As she jumped out, she was playing the song in her mind; *I'll never be lonely…* She grabbed the wig and glasses from the front seat and jammed them into the dumpster, then pulled off the smock and sang, "Never be lonely anymore." She tossed it in.

She walked around the car, cracking all the windows a couple of inches and calling to Heather, "Back in a moment, honey." She hurried into the store and bought a box of donuts caked in powdered sugar. Back outside, she threw her pocket book in the trunk, jumped into the car and began chomping a donut, spilling sugar on her pants, as she drove. She turned onto a dirt road, heading toward Amalia, a tiny berg just a few miles from the Colorado line.

Heather still slept. A sleeping baby, a back road where no cops would ever patrol, getting closer to home—she should be feeling really happy, but she needed a baby fix.

She pulled into a turnout and shut off the engine. Climbing into the back seat, she scooted over beside Heather. "Ba-by," she whispered. "Baby." She touched the infant's chin, and Heather woke, raising tiny arms over her head. "Hello, little one. My, you have pretty blue eyes." Melody cupped Heather's cheek in her palm, as tears flowed down her own cheeks. "I love you, and I'll protect you, little girl." She lingered with the child a while, but that antsy feeling made her move on.

Looking up at the sky, she said, "I have faith in you again, Lord. I'd almost lost it, but now I know you had this plan for me."

Back behind the wheel, she turned down the radio and adjusted the mirror so she could see the sweet little girl's face. They passed an isolated ranch, and the road narrowed, as it entered a forest—with huge pine trees and clusters of aspen. Water gushed from a hillside and ran beneath the road, and she glimpsed a rippling stream in the valley below.

That shrink from back in high school, Dr. Hoskins, had said that it was natural for her to feel a little crazy after her tragedy. She'd only been a sophomore and lived with just her nutty, bible-toting mom. The shrink had told Melody to try to get past her setbacks and to give herself credit every time she made a move to improve her life.

Now, four years later and a month after the second heartbreak, she'd followed Dr. Hoskins' advice and taken a huge step. Heather was proof of that. So what if she'd forgotten one little detail? On *Law and Order* those parking lot cameras didn't work half of the time anyway.

She took a deep breath and looked back at Heather. "When you're older, we'll have a picnic right here in this forest, and I'll tell you about the day you were born to me." The wheel vibrated and the car shook. She looked ahead and saw that they were barrel-assing off the road toward a grove of bushes and trees. She'd missed a damn curve.

Melody hit the brakes, skidding. She braced against the wheel and heard a boom, as the Escort bounded through a ditch. Her chest smacked the wheel, horn blasting. Her body flew backward, bouncing her noggin against the head rest. Clinging to the wheel, she jabbed her foot at the brake pedal but missed. She steered past a few huge trees and a thicket of shrubbery. Branches slashed the windows, as the car veered into the bushes that blocked the gully ahead.

Damn it, this isn't fair, she thought, as the Escort's left side sank, and the car ground to a halt.

Chapter 2

Heather began to bawl.

Melody glanced back, seeing the infant still strapped in the baby seat. Melody's head throbbed, and her ribs ached. Through her side window she saw only leaves and branches pressed against the glass. But the passenger side looked clear. The radio was still playing—some country and western tune.

She ignored the noise and the pain in her body, moving toward her little girl. Climbing over the brake lever in the center, she cracked open the passenger door. The song was cut off by a male announcer's voice. "Sorry to interrupt that great Tammy Wynette tune, but we have an Amber Alert. Authorities in northern New Mexico and southern Colorado are searching for a baby girl, Shirley Cavendish, abducted this morning from Santa Fe Mercy Hospital."

Melody couldn't breathe. 'Shirley' had been the name on the bassinet at the hospital, but the cops couldn't know about Melody...

"The baby has blond hair and blue eyes," the DJ continued. "She weighs 7 pounds 9 ounces and is 19 inches long. Police are looking for a beige 1989 Ford Escort, Colorado license AY541B and a suspect named Melody Reeves."

Melody gasped.

"Ms. Reeves is a resident of Alamosa, Colorado, described as 20 years old, Caucasian, 5 foot 6 inches tall, weighing 140 pounds, with brown eyes and brown hair but last seen wearing a blond wig." *Shit.* Melody stared at the radio, her heartbeat pounding in her temples and her gut aching, like she'd just been in a second accident and the steering wheel had caught her square in the stomach this time.

She turned off the ignition, silencing the radio. Melody stashed the key ring in her shirt pocket and turned to see the baby's eyes clamped shut, mouth open wide, feet kicking, as she screamed.

She couldn't let herself get mad at the baby. "It's all right, little girl. We're going to find a way." She swung the passenger door open, smacking it into the dirt leaving an opening of only a few inches. A spasm ripped through her bruised ribs, as she kicked hard with both feet. The door gave another inch. She braced her hands against the driver's seat, grunted and kicked, opening the door just far enough.

Melody squeezed through, clambered along the side of a dirt mound and opened the back door. She un-strapped Heather from the baby seat and hugged her. "You look fine, baby girl; not hurt at all."

Wincing at the pressure on her ribs, she held Heather close and sat in the dirt. She eyed the Escort, wondering if the car would ever run again, and who could she find to fix it way out here? And would she dare drive it, anyway, with the cops after her? Little Heather squirmed, resting her head on Melody's arm. She let the baby's essence comfort her, as she thought about what to do.

After a while, she said, "Heather dear, Mommy's going to go find new license plates for our car, and then pretty soon, we'll get a brand new car... and Mommy's going to play a game. It's called 'Musical Names.' We already changed your name from that geeky 'Shirley' to glamorous 'Heather.' She held Heather's hand between her own thumb and forefinger and shook it. "Congratulations on your new name. And now I'll change mine to … 'Siena—Siena NewHeart,' because my new little girl has given me a new and better heart. I don't know how, but you and I will turn everything around and live like princesses in a dream castle."

———

Melody—no, Siena—didn't know how long she and the baby had been sitting there, and then Heather's crying roused her. She unfastened the infant's diaper tab and peeked inside. "Your diapie doesn't look

6

wet," she said. "And I don't smell a stinky. So Mommy will get your bottle and formula." She got up and slid Heather into the baby seat.

The branches of a large red-barked bush swallowed up the left side of the Escort. Siena unlocked the trunk and tried to pull it open, but the branches held it down. She burrowed under them, pressed her body as far as she could and heaved. "OWWWW." Sliding out, she paced back and forth. *I've got to get the friggin' trunk open,* she thought. She grasped one of the smaller boughs and yanked; it bowed but didn't snap. She dug her heals into the gravelly soil and pulled harder, using all of her strength, but she lost her footing and fell. The stalk snapped back in place as if she hadn't touched it.

Hopeless. And the baby formula and all the things Siena needed, like her wallet and her cell phone, were locked in the trunk. She leaned into the back seat and patted Heather's cheek. "I'm trying to work this out. Please be quiet." The baby screamed louder. "Heather!" *Time to leave before I get out-of-control mad,* she thought. "Mommy has to leave you to go find help."

At least the car was in a shady spot. Siena rolled down the back windows a couple of inches. She locked the doors, closing her baby in safe and sound, and walked to the road.

She'd driven miles since seeing that last ranch, so Siena turned up the road, feeling achy and fretful and muttering, "God why have you made this so terribly hard for me. All I wanted was a child to love, to make up for what You did to me." She thought about what Dr. Hoskins might say if he saw her now. *You fucked up, girl.* No, not the doctor; that was her mother talking. She'd always been unlucky—given a screw-up for a mom, getting the fucked up name, Melody, her two terrible losses and now her car run off the road. *God damn it. Can't think that way. Can't use those words. Sorry, God. I know you're just testing me.*

She almost walked past the dirt driveway that wound back into the forest. There was no mail box, but that didn't mean much; the post office wouldn't deliver way back here in the woods. There were tire marks in the sand. Following the drive as it meandered between pine trees, Siena spotted a small house sided in natural brown wood. It had a porch on one side and a shed further back in the woods with a beat-up red pickup nearby. "Hello," she called. She took a few steps and called louder. No answer. Who lived in a place like this? On *Criminal Minds*, her favorite Wednesday night show, some sort of pervert rapist would jump out wielding a cleaver.

The porch held one wooden wide-backed rocking chair, its white paint stained and peeling. She stepped onto the porch and heard a squeak. Flinching, she almost ran, but it was just a loose board. Siena peered through the grimy window, but a ratty curtain kept her from seeing inside. She knocked on the door, noticing that it had two dead bolts. She called out again, banged hard on the door and tried to open it. No luck. She stepped off the porch and walked around the house and out to the shed. The door stood ajar.

"Anyone in there?" she called.

Easing the door open, she saw a bare light bulb on the ceiling with a string hanging down. She pulled it, and the light came on. The place was a mess, with yard tools crammed in one corner and cob-web-shrouded wooden boxes in another. But to her right, she spotted a work table with built-in cubby-holes behind. This area was neat.

Some of the slots held lengths of pipe. In others there were jars with labels—the closest one said "Nitrate." A little rack held screw-drivers, pliers and a small soldering iron. Strips of wire were lined up neatly on a shelf, and there was a jar holding little springs and various metal gadgets. Was the owner some sort of plumber or electrician?

Fighting the urge to get the hell out, Siena stepped to the area with the gardening tools. She pushed aside a shovel and pickax, and behind she found a couple of hand-saws. She picked up a saw, rummaged around and found a long-handled clipper.

BAM!

Siena flinched.

Was someone shooting? An explosion in the house?

She turned off the light, moved to the door of the shed and waited, grasping the tools really, really tight. She peered out, took a deep breath and took off running.

Chapter 3

Wendell had almost blown himself to bits. But this had been the best detonation so far, and he smiled as he strode toward the cabin. Then he spotted the alarm light in the back window. Someone had been—or was—on the property. He tensed and ran toward the back door, unbolted the padlock and stepped inside. Rushing through the main room, past the worn, brown sofa and armchair, he told himself it was probably nothing. But daytime alarms were rare, and if someone had wandered onto his property during his explosives test, it could mean disaster. He checked the front door and window, ran through the bedroom and checked there, then turned back to the living room bookcases, the beat-up, cluttered desk and the rack of electronic equipment—no disturbance anywhere. But he hadn't locked the work shed! Grabbing his shotgun from the corner, he broke it open to make sure the load was in, banged it shut and went outside. He'd fire it into the air—that would scare almost anyone.

At the shed, he listened for a moment before gripping the door handle and yanking it open. No one there. He examined the jars with their precious powders and crystals, all the tools and implements. All right. Maybe a false alarm—a bird flying past one of the sensors or a deer walking by...

Back in the cabin, Wendell sat at the desk and cued the video on his surveillance system. Four pictures appeared on the divided computer monitor. He used the mouse to cue rewind. First he saw himself in the bottom right-hand quadrant. Bearded, tall and lanky, in his red checked shirt and blue jeans, he jerked backward across the screen in the fast rewind.

Within a minute the image of a young woman appeared on the top left screen. He slowed the rewind and kept watching until the woman—more of a girl really—first appeared. Wendell hit play and watched the stranger stalk down the driveway toward the cabin. He minimized the other three pictures and filled the screen with her image—not a bad-looking girl, a nice, rounded body, and she had a pretty, pouty sort of face—kind of like Doris back in high school. But Wendell had learned a harsh lesson from Doris the snob, and this girl was trespassing on his property.

He saw the way her eyes flitted here and there, looking almost frantic before she turned away from the cabin. Wendell restored the other three quadrants and saw her reappear in the top right corner. She wore light blue slacks and a short-sleeved pink blouse, and she didn't look like a deputy scoping for a pot farm or, worse, like FBI. Still, his gut constricted, as he saw her rush to his work shed and sneak inside. He held his breath and observed a couple of minutes until she appeared in the doorway and then took off like a bandit with one of Wendell's saws and his long-handled branch cutter.

So she's one of them; thieves and swindlers, Wendell thought.

He hauled the shotgun out to the red Dodge pickup and jumped in. A minute later he was out of the driveway, doing 50 on the dirt road toward Cimarron, clenching his teeth, as he slid around a curve. There ahead—the thieving girl stood beside the road, holding her hands, and his stolen goods, behind her.

Wendell skidded to a stop, set the brake and slid to the passenger side of the pickup. He glanced at her, noticed her insolent look, brown eyes staring, as if she'd done nothing wrong. He noticed her full breasts too, tight against the pink blouse, as he lowered his eyes.

He swallowed and said, "Give me back my saw and lopper."

Chapter 4

Holding her sore ribs with one hand and swinging the saw and clipper in the other, Siena rushed along the deserted road. She heard a vehicle coming up behind, coming fast from the sound of it. None of the larger pine trees was close by, no place to hide.

She turned and held the tools behind her, watching an old red pickup—the one from the cabin—tear around the bend, hearing the engine cut back. *Damn.* The cabin's owner might somehow sense that she'd been on his property, but he couldn't know what she'd taken. The pickup slowed, and Siena took a deep breath.

The pickup stopped beside her, and she got a look, as the guy slid across to her side of the truck. A scary dude with a thick dirty-brown beard, he wore a red plaid shirt. He glared at her for a moment, his dark, shaggy eyebrows meeting in the center, but then his eyes fled downward, over her body and settled on the ground.

"Give me back my saw and lopper," he said.

Crap, he knew. *Lopper* must be what they called the long handled clipper she was hiding behind her. There was no point denying she had the tools. Siena trembled, as she brought them out and held them at her side. She shook her head. "I can't."

The man glanced at her again. He scratched his beard then dropped his hand back to his side, then picked it up and scratched again. *This guy's more scared than I am,* she thought. *Doesn't have the balls to look me in the eye.*

"You can't steal a person's tools."

"I don't have time for this, Mister. There was no one at your shitty cabin, and I borrowed them, OK?" She turned and began walking again.

He pulled the pickup forward and veered to the side of the road, cutting her off. He swung the door open, and she gripped the saw tighter, ready to take a swing at his head. But he stayed in the truck. "You can't do this; it's wrong." He spoke toward her, making eye contact with her boobs for a second but not her face. "And don't swear at me. I don't like it," he said.

Obviously a perv, she thought. But this one seemed pretty tame. "Then give me a ride. I had an accident and my baby's in the car. Take me there and give me a hand, and you'll get these back."

The man considered for a moment and then nodded. "I believe in helping people." He slid across to the driver's side.

Siena climbed in, gripping the saw in her right hand. She wondered about the way he spoke—more like a bizarro boy scout than a sexual deviant.

The windows on both sides were open, but she smelled the man's B.O., B.O. and something sharp, like the smell of a gunshot—the explosion she'd heard. His hands were dirty with black grit caked under the nails. "My name's …Siena," she said.

The guy didn't respond. He backed up, jammed the lever into *Drive*, spinning the tires on the dirt road, accelerating. He didn't look at her as they cruised.

"Better slow down," she said. "My car went off the road on a turn like the one coming up… somewhere… here." She scanned the roadside. When she glanced at the guy, he was eying her, and then he looked back to the road—creepy.

"There. Back up."

As the truck rolled backward, she pointed to a spot where the roadside berm was scraped. "Stop."

———

Wendell popped the truck into 4-wheel drive and eased it over the low mound, through a ditch, into the forest. He followed the skid marks this crazy girl had laid down when she ran off the road. Edging past a cluster of pine trees, he spotted a little beige car, one side buried in the bushes—so she hadn't lied about the accident. "You really jammed it in there," he said.

The girl—Siena—jumped out before he'd stopped the truck, and he watched her run to the car, unlock it and retrieve a bawling baby from the back seat—telling the truth about that too. As he climbed out of the truck, Siena gestured toward the back of her car. "The baby's food is in the trunk. You *gotta* help me get it."

Seeing this girl-woman with the tiny kid, Wendell got a warm feeling inside. But this Siena girl had invaded his sanctuary, and, if she was so anxious to get the kid's food, why hadn't she folded down the back seat and crawled in? The answer was simple; this was one wild-eyed nut of a girl who hadn't thought of something so easy, who was prepared to fight Wendell with his own saw to get what her kid needed. He walked toward her. "You know you could have…"

"She's really hungry. Grab the saw and help me here."

He walked to the car's open back door. "I was going to suggest folding down the seat." He eyed the baby seat, spotted a buckle on the belt that held it in place, unfastened it and removed it.

The girl was right at his side, holding the baby. "Oh, God. Why didn't I think to do that? Heather, I'm sorry! Set the baby seat over there, Mister. You haven't told me your name."

Wendell put the seat on the dirt a few feet from the car, and the girl laid her baby in it. She gave Wendell a hard stare. "Don't touch her; she's very sensitive."

"It's Wendell."

"All right, don't touch her, Wendell." Siena bent into the car, clicked the catch and folded down the back seat.

Behind Wendell, the baby began to cry, but he ignored it, watching the way her shirt rode up, as she bent to reach into the trunk. She pulled out a couple of blankets and tossed them into the front of the car. Then she stretched out across the folded-down seat-back and began squirming through the opening into the trunk. It had been so long since he'd been this close to a woman, been able to watch her body move and stretch. The truth was that he'd only seen magazines and films; never an actual woman's buttocks this intimate way with her pale blue pants riding up into the crack, the fabric showing the line of her underpants. A thrilling tingle zipped from Wendell's penis to his testicles. He stared, as Siena crawled backwards, now, her blouse hiking up, so he could see the skin of her back. She bent to the left, and two little bulges of fat formed on that side, but the other side was smooth and taught. The indentation of her backbone reminded him of the sensuous curve of a DNA helix.

"Wendell, are you ogling me?"

He took a step back and looked away, not able to lie by denying it, not able to answer at all. Embarrassed and aroused and thinking about the way Siena could jeopardize everything, Wendell headed for his truck. He called back to her. "I'll saw away some of these branches." It wouldn't take him long to free her car from most of the brush. Then he'd take her someplace to call the Auto Club or some garage and be done with her.

He took the chain saw and ear mufflers from the metal chest in the back of the pickup. He put on the hearing protection, fired up the saw and noticed the way the young woman was feeding the infant with the bottle and the way she turned the baby away to protect it from the noise. Revving the saw, he cut the branches from the back of the Escort. When he finished, he idled the saw and observed Siena; she had the baby strapped to her chest now in a pale green sling with daisies embroidered on it.

Wendell thought again of his dates with Doris, back in high school, taking her to the movies and making out in the back seat of his dad's car. That was the last time he'd been alone with a good-looking female—20 years ago. He remembered too, the anguish he'd felt when Doris had broken it off, saying that she'd had a good time with him, but she'd met another boy who wasn't so strange. And Wendell had gone without a word, the way he'd always retreated in life.

Siena looked up from the baby, and Wendell headed to the front of the car. He sawed away branches, wanting to gain access to the engine, fix the car, winch it free and send this nuisance on her way.

Chapter 5

Wendell found Siena sitting against the car's trunk, the baby secured to her chest in the green sling. The baby made a glugging sound and spit white, mucous-y liquid onto the girl's shoulder.

Siena dabbed at the mess with a cloth and glanced his way.

Wendell dropped his gaze. "I got the branches clear and took a look into your engine."

"So can you fix my crappy car?"

He disliked the word *crappy*, but he let it pass. "There's a small forest inside your engine compartment. Branches are lodged in your fan belt. They've tipped the battery at an angle and pulled distributor wires loose. The fuel line may be ruptured, so I can't use the chain saw under there."

"But you can fix it?" Her eyes pleaded with him.

"Afraid not. You need a mechanic."

"Wendell, I tried my cell phone, but there's no reception. Drive me up to Amalia, so I can make some calls."

He let out the breath he'd been holding, relieved that she hadn't asked to go to his cabin. "Sure. I want to help you out... Siena."

———

Siena sat on the passenger side of the pickup, one hand gripping the door handle and the other steadying the baby seat in the center. Her cute little babe was asleep again. If Siena used her cell phone, when they got to Amalia, the cops could track her, grab her up and try to take her girl. She kept an eye on Heather as she pulled her phone out of her bag, flipped it open and turned it off. "Wendell, my battery's dead. Do you have a cell phone?"

"Nope."

Amalia turned out to be a tiny nothing without even a decent store, let alone a pay phone. "That's OK," she told him. "The sign says Costilla's just a few miles ahead." That would take them closer to Colorado, closer to the tidy apartment she'd have to abandon to avoid the cops.

"Wendell, have you ever had something taken from you, something precious?"

She thought she saw the hint of a nod, and she asked, "Do you have any friends to confide in? I tell my friend, Millie, about my sorrows." Siena felt tears form in her eyes and wondered if she was gaining any sympathy. "Do you ever question why God lets wicked things happen?"

"No God in it," Wendell said. "Men took what I lost."

"How can you look at this sleeping baby, Wendell, and not understand? God made her and gave her to me. God makes everything happen." Siena wanted to go on, but she was choking up, flashing back to the sad memories of her losses and then remembering the days when her mom and that phony minister had shouted all that Jesus BS at her. 'Jesus is Lord. Jesus is the Word. You're a sinner. Pray to Jesus. Jesus. Jesus.' She had realized then that people who spoke His holy name the loudest showed the least love for their fellow humans. And then Siena had retreated to the forest on a magical day when she hadn't felt the least bit afraid to wander, not scared of bears or wolves. As she sat on a boulder by a flowing stream, rays of sunshine, beaming down through the trees, found her shoulder. God's hand warmed her. His message of compassion filled her, and she decided to speak directly to Him and hear only His gentle words from then on.

In Costilla, Wendell drove up the main street, passing a Shamrock gas station and a funky sort of trading post. Siena ducked at the sight of a cop car. *Rats.* The sudden move must have looked suspicious; she needed an excuse. Her face was close to Heather's, so she tickled the baby's tummy. Heather opened her eyes, made a face and wiggled her shoulders. "Good girl. Pretty baby," Siena said.

She sat up again. "Did you see her, Wendell? Heather waved to me and gave me a beautiful smile."

"Infants that young don't smile." Wendell was drumming his fingers on the steering wheel—nervous, annoyed, or maybe suspicious?

They passed a sign that said "San Luis, Colorado 23." From San Luis it was only an hour to Alamosa. She needed to get home to visit her apartment, maybe for the last time, elude the cops and go in to pick up some of her things.

Wendell slowed the truck and made a U-turn. "I haven't seen any pay phones, but I bet they'll let you make a call from the store." He pulled into the parking lot.

Siena thought again about the cop car and the other cops who might be swarming her apartment by now. Soon they'd be heading for her bank to choke off her money. But they'd need a court order, wouldn't they? She had to get Wendell to take her to the ATM in San Luis.

Siena's throat constricted, as she eyed him. "Wendell, I'll only be a minute." She reached over and pulled the keys out of the ignition.

Wendell pointed an accusing finger at her. "You don't need to…"

"Keep an eye on Heather for me." She gave him a stern look, noticing that he was chewing his lower lip. "I'll be watching you, Wendell."

"I won't touch her." He edged away from the baby, pressing his side against the truck door. "But…"

She jumped out of the truck and entered the store, seeing shelves of canned goods and snack foods. The clerk was a woman, shorter than Siena and dark—Native American. Siena didn't eye the ceiling for cameras and didn't look at the clerk, as she passed the counter. She peeked out of the window, assuring herself that Wendell was still in the driver's seat of his truck, still pressed against his door, not molesting Heather.

She pretended to scan the cookie section and then returned to the pickup. "Sorry, Wendell, there's no pay phone, and the bitch that runs the store wouldn't let me…" She took in her companion's frown, and said, "That's right, you don't like curse words. The shrew wouldn't let me use the phone, even when I told her I'd had an accident. And, anyway, we need to go on to San Luis."

Wendell pouched his cheek, opened his mouth and closed it, opened it again—all the while focused on the dashboard. "But…"

"Don't worry; I'll pay for the gas." She saw that he had leaned back, staring up at the ceiling, rubbing his hands together. "Wendell, you told me you wanted to help me out; those were your words. I have to go to San Luis and get money from my bank, so I can pay for a tow truck. It's not far."

He sighed, blinked, glanced at her and turned back to the road. Pulling out of the lot, he headed north on New Mexico 522, but then Heather began bawling, and he pulled over.

Wendell jumped out of the truck, and paced the dirt shoulder with his hands in his pockets. Siena fed her little girl and burped her, and then the smell told her that the baby needed changing.

When she finished and Heather quieted down, Wendell climbed back into the driver's seat. "You look uncomfortable," she said. "Didn't you ever have a baby brother or sister?"

"I was an only child." He drove back onto the highway, and within a few minutes they were in a wide agricultural valley in southern Colorado, and after another 20 they entered San Luis, a place with real stores and that ice cream parlor they were passing. She would have loved some Rocky Road, but figured she'd pushed Wendell far enough. "Wendell, how can you live way out in nowhere?"

"It's not a problem."

"Look at San Luis; it's a nice town. I couldn't survive like you do, without people, without restaurants and stores."

They drove past a building that said "Visitor Center," and Siena cringed; right beneath that sign, another said "Police Station." "Turn here. My bank's down this block."

Once she took money from the ATM, the cops would know she was in town. She couldn't let them find out she was traveling in their red pickup, which meant they'd better not drive by the ATM with its camera. "Pull into that lot by the drugstore."

Funny, she'd been thinking about it as *their* vehicle, like she and Wendell were a couple. But they weren't, and here was Heather between them on the seat, and Siena had to leave her a second time with this stranger. She had no choice. "You got a hat and a pair of sunglasses, Wendell?"

He took the keys out of the ignition and pulled a grubby, wrinkled, green John Deere cap from behind the seat. She got her first good look at his eyes, as he stared at her for all of three seconds. They were almost as blue as Heather's. "You're a fugitive, aren't you, Siena?" he asked.

"No, Wendell, I'm sensitive to the sun, that's all."

"I don't have sun glasses."

"OK." She held out her hand, palm up. Wendell hesitated and then handed over his keys.

Chapter 6

Tugging the John Deere cap low over her eyes, Siena punched her code into the ATM and checked her bank balance—$348.52. She tried to withdraw $340, but the screen lit up with *Amount Exceeds Daily Limit*. Crap. Had the cops already shut her down? She fought the urge to get the hell out of there.

She half-remembered that there might be a daily limit, and it could be... She punched in $300, and the screen said *Processing Your Request*. It spit the money out, and she stuffed it into her pocket book.

Hustling back to the drugstore parking lot, she sighed in relief at the sight of the red pickup, with Wendell in the driver's seat.

Pulling out her cell phone, she walked to the side of the drugstore and watched the red pickup. She dialed and then heard the familiar voice; "Hello."

"Hi, Millie, it's Melody. Is there..."

"What's going on, Melody? The cops came asking about you, and they acted real pissed off."

"Are any there now?"

"Any...?"

"Cops, Millie. Are the cops there?"

"I turned on the TV, and there was a news flash. Melody, did you steal someone's baby?"

Siena saw Wendell getting out of the pickup. He stood for a moment looking in at the front seat—at Heather. What was he up to? "Millie, you can't believe I'd take a baby that wasn't mine."

"No, but..."

Siena had to get back to the truck to prevent Wendell from doing anything stupid—like what if he had another set of keys, and he left

21

Heather in the parking lot and drove off. He was pacing in front of the drugstore, looking perturbed.

"The cops, Millie, have they left?"

"I think so, but they were all over here an hour ago—uniforms out in back of the apartment building and two suits in my face asking questions. Melody, they said the FBI is coming."

Siena's gut lurched. She had to convince Wendell to take her home to Alamosa. If the cops were gone, and if the FBI hadn't arrived, she could sneak in and gather a few of her things. She really needed her camera to take the baby's first pictures and the nice second-hand crib that she had sitting in her living room and the mobile with the dangling bunnies and carrots.

"Listen, Millie. Do me a favor. Run over to the auto parts store and pick up my paycheck." Siena watched Wendell circle his truck, look into the cab and wander into the drugstore, leaving Heather alone!

Millie gasped. "Christ no, Siena. Did you hear what I said about the cops? They told me to let them know if I hear from you."

Millie had turned really crappy all of a sudden, but Siena needed her. "I get it; you're scared. But at least you can check something for me. Wait a half an hour and walk around the apartment house to see if they've got eyes on the place. Carry a bag of garbage, so you have an excuse to go out to the back alley. I'll call in an hour, and you can fill me in."

"I don't know, Melody. What have you gone and done?"

Siena saw Wendell walk out of the store, scratching at his beard the way he had when she'd first met him. He was nervous as hell, and she couldn't afford to let him stew. "I don't have time for this, Millie. Walk around the apartment; that's all I ask. I'll call you in an hour." She clicked the phone shut, shoved it in her bag and hurried back to the pickup.

Chapter 7

Special Agent David Webster wondered why he was so annoyed to be working with Agent Cecil Bates. Bates worked hard and seemed eager for approval. But guys like Bates, who talked all the time, had a way of interrupting a man's logic. They dragged everything out, slowed the work, and delay could prove fatal as hell in a kidnapping case.

As he drove from Albuquerque to Cimarron, Webster had wanted time to sift his memories. He'd needed to wallow in his guilt about that first abduction so long before and to grieve a bit for that long-ago kidnapped infant. *Christ,* he thought, *if only Bates would shut up.*

Webster drove the dark green Ford Explorer into the parking lot of the Cimarron General Store. Bates jumped out, hustled to the porch and glad-handed a couple of guys in beige sheriff's uniforms.

After easing out of the Explorer, Webster approached the three men. Bates held up some clear plastic bags. "Lookie what these sheriff's men found—this has gotta be the disguise that Melody woman wore in the kidnapping."

Bates was a skinny runt of a man who acted like an eager puppy bringing the newspaper to his master. And who could respect a man named Cecil who said *lookie* when he got excited?

Webster took the bags and examined each—black-framed glasses, a blonde wig and yellow nurse's blouse. There was no doubt that Melody Reeves had come through Cimarron and discarded these on her way to where? Home to Colorado, most likely. If she'd gone there, case over. And, please, Jesus, let the baby be unharmed.

"Pretty good evidence, don't you think?" Bates said. "Oh, this is Deputy Graves and Sergeant Sanchez. Fellas, meet my partner, Dave Webster."

23

Webster glowered at Bates and shook the deputies' hands.

Deputy Graves was a six foot tall Anglo with a bushy brown mustache and a scar across his left cheek. He held a spiral notepad in his left hand. He'd be the organized one. "Have you found witnesses to Ms. Reeves' activities here in Cimarron?" Webster asked.

"The man who owns this store." Deputy Graves waved a hand at the building's front door. "He saw a picture of the suspect on TV and called us in. We showed him the photo, and he confirmed that Melody Reeves bought a box of sugar donuts here this morning."

Bates pointed at the bags in Webster's hand. "The deputies found those in a dumpster around back. But there were no witnesses to the woman tossing them in."

Webster eyed Deputy Graves. "What time did she purchase the donuts?"

Graves glanced at his notepad. "10:45 AM, about a half hour before the owner saw the Amber Alert on TV. If he hadn't called us, we'd have had no idea she even came through Cimarron."

"Did you men take a detailed statement from the storekeeper?" Webster asked. "And can you run a canvas? Find out if anyone else saw the woman or noticed a beige Escort near the store or driving through town."

Deputy Graves nodded. "Yes, sir and yes, sir."

"Any cameras inside the store or out here?" Webster glanced up under the porch roof.

"No, too bad, ain't it?" Deputy Graves said. "We're a small town, don't have that much crime."

"Don't let anyone near the dumpster," Webster said. "And don't touch it any more than you already have."

Sergeant Sanchez grimaced, and Webster wondered if Sanchez resented him because of his color or just because he was FBI. No time to worry about petty bigotry. "We'll send someone up from Albuquerque to take finger prints. In the store too; tell the owner to close. Treat it as a crime scene, starting now."

The other men followed, as Webster approached the vehicle. "We're going to drive north, assuming the suspect is heading for familiar ground. We'll return after we apprehend her and go over your statements."

Sergeant Sanchez took a step toward Webster and held out his hand. He was a powerfully built Latino, and he wore an angry frown. "We need to take those evidence bags back to the station."

Webster tensed. "It's a kidnapping, so it's FBI jurisdiction. That's all you need to know, Deputy. If that's not enough, Ms. Reeves resides in Colorado. By now, she's crossed the state line. It's our case no matter how you look at it."

Sergeant Sanchez didn't back away. "We need to go to the station to log those off the Cimarron Sheriffs' books and make them FBI responsibility. It's called chain of custody—something we small town cops do, Special Agent Webster." His emphasis on Webster's title was like a wad of spit in the eye, but Webster figured maybe he'd deserved it.

———

Back inside the Explorer, with the evidence in the trunk, Webster stewed about how to deal with Bates. Bates had been around for six months, so Webster shouldn't have to explain that FBI agents don't treat local cops as equals, don't confide in local cops, don't talk like fucking hillbillies.

Hold the anger in. You're in charge here. If you treat this young fool with something close to respect, some day he might deserve it.

But Webster couldn't piss around with nice-guy BS while Melody Reeves was fleeing.

Bates had a map spread across the dash board, tracing his right forefinger over it. "I figure since that Melody chick came through Cimarron, she's taking back roads, instead of making a beeline for home. From here she'll head up New Mexico 204 through Amalia and then maybe to San Francisco, Colorado. Who'd have guessed they'd have a San Francisco in Colorado?"

"I suppose this Route 204 is one of New Mexico's fine rutted dirt thoroughfares."

"Good deduction, partner." Bates grinned.

Peeling out of the parking lot and heading toward the highway, Webster took a deep breath and counted to three, but it didn't help. "On this case and in this car, you are my subordinate, not my partner, Agent Bates. And don't refer to the suspect by her first name. That could lead people, like those Cimarron back-water New Mexico deputies, to think that the Bureau has sympathy for the nutty bitch. And stop acting like a kiss-ass who doesn't belong in the FB fucking I."

Bates straightened in his seat. "Whatever you say, Dave. I'll call her nutty bitch from now on, to keep everything professional."

Chapter 8

When Wendell balked at the idea of heading to Alamosa, Siena almost peed her pants. They couldn't sit in his truck, less than a block from the bank. "Wendell, we have to get out of here."

He gave her a funny look. "What's wrong?"

Her heart was racing. "We can talk, but not here."

Wendell started the truck. He was scratching himself again—first his side and then his thigh—as he drove to a neighborhood a few blocks off San Luis' main street. He parked in front of a yellow-and-white '60s era bungalow and stared at the dashboard. "I drove you to Amalia, to Costilla and here to San Luis. That's enough."

Siena had grown used to his B.O., but his attitude pissed her off. She watched three 12-year-old boys tossing a football in the street a half a block away, as she tried to develop a strategy. The boys took turns, one of them backing up, preparing to throw the ball, as another ran a zigzag pattern and then tried to catch the pass. "It'll only take another hour to Alamosa, and I said I'd supply the gas. Look, I'll pay to fill your entire tank and give you another twenty bucks."

Wendell held his two hands on the steering wheel, shaking his head. "You got your money out of the bank, so you can pay to rent a car or call a garage to help you. I'm heading back to New Mexico."

"You lied when you said you wanted to help me." She touched his hand, but he still gazed straight ahead, like she hadn't spoken. "You're a bastard, Wendell."

He shot her a malevolent look. "I wanted to help, but I saw the way you reacted to that trooper back in Costilla. And you used my John Deere hat to disguise yourself."

27

"I gave the flippin' hat back—there, I didn't swear; are you happy? Is that what's bothering you, I soiled your crummy hat?"

"I really would help you but ..." Sweat broke out on Wendell's forehead, and his eyes blinked a few times. "I just can't. Whatever you're hiding from, I can't let the police find me with you. I'll leave you here in San Luis."

He looked up, and he must have seen the fear on her face. "OK. Look. I'll drop you anywhere between here and Amalia."

Wendell's statement about the police finding him intrigued her. But then she heard a smack and looked up to see the football bounding from the street onto the lawn of the yellow and white house. A kid with wavy-brown hair, in a blue and white football shirt, scooped up the ball, glanced at her and stared. The kid turned toward his buddies and shouted, "Hey, it's that lady on TV—the one that stole the baby."

Siena turned toward Wendell, about to tell him to drive away, but he'd already fired up the pickup. The kid was yelling to his friends, but Siena couldn't hear over the roar of the engine. The truck peeled rubber and flew past the other two boys, around a corner, to the main drag and out of town. The truck's movement pressed her against the door, and her side ached, but that was trivial compared to the pain in her head.

―――

Siena glanced at Wendell, as he drove, saw him chewing his lip, his eyes narrowed in a look that said I'm-trying-to-be-patient. If he was a normal guy, he wouldn't understand about her and Heather; he'd head for that police station in the San Luis Visitor Center. Then she'd have to scratch his eyes out, grab Heather and bolt. But Wendell was fleeing. "Slow down if you don't want to be pulled over," she said. He shot her a quick, worried glance and let up on the gas. The speedometer needle dropped to just under the 35mph speed limit.

Wendell wasn't normal; that was no news. But she could think of only two reasons why he'd drive off with her this way. He was taking her somewhere to rape and kill her, or he was just as scared of the cops as she was. She saw the way he eyed her boobs, but he also went along with almost everything she told him to do. If he pulled over and started to drop trou', she'd tell him where to stick his dick, and he'd probably try to do it.

He turned the Dodge pickup onto a two-lane road following a sign for Chama and sped up to 60. Siena hadn't heard of a Chama, Colorado, but she knew from the mountains looming in the distance that Wendell was driving her away from Alamosa. "Let me explain why I need to go home, Wendell. Let me explain everything."

"The next time I stop, you'll get out of this truck, and take her with you." He tilted his head toward Heather, who was wiggling her shoulders back and forth. She said, "oog-oog, oog-oog."

Siena couldn't breathe for a second, overcome by joy at the baby's first real utterance, but she had to deal with Wendell. "You—you monster—how could you throw a baby out in this wilderness?"

Wendell turned right at an intersection, now heading for San Pablo. Then he swung the pickup onto a gravel road, passing grassland and thickets of small trees, heading for a stone mountain range in the distance.

Wendell pulled off onto a dirt turn-out. He glared at her, still working his jaw. His furious blue eyes bore into her. Spittle dripped from one corner of his mouth, disappearing into his disheveled beard, and he scratched his thighs with both hands. "You stole her from her mother, and you dare call me a monster."

This wasn't a man intent on rape; it was a 40-year-old Boy Scout. "I didn't.... She's mine." Siena's heart beat wild in her chest, and tears ran from her eyes. "You told me before that you lost something precious. What did you lose, Wendell?"

———

Wendell could overpower this despicable girl-woman and force her out of the truck. He could take the baby and leave it someplace where people would find it. But the girl would fight, and he'd have to hurt her. He imagined pounding a fist into her turned-up nose, and felt ashamed. He clawed at his beard with the hand that wanted to punch her.

Maybe Siena had some reason for taking the baby, like the reasons he had for his own socially condemned actions. She was asking about his loss, as if she cared about him, and now she touched his thigh. That tingle came again, and this time it was a pleasing warm stream running up his leg to tickle his scrotum. Was he going crazy?

His throat constricted with fury. What had he lost; he couldn't have answered her question, if he'd wanted to.

"Wendell," she said. "I see that angry look on your face, and it hurts me. I-I had two babies that God meant to give me, but something happened, and I lost them." She sobbed the last words, wiping away tears with her finger tips. "Miscarriages, Wendell."

In the days when he'd been around people, all their talk had made him indecisive and weak. Now, living alone with his books and his thoughts and his project, he'd become a man of purpose. And now this girl challenged his resolve. "What you did was … inexcusable."

"It was God's will, Wendell. God took my babies. I screamed curses at Him, but He told me there was a mistake in the way I was made." Siena's right hand pressed against her left side, as she rocked the baby carrier with the other hand. "God said I should search for my child. And I realized… He'd put my baby in another woman's belly. I found her there in the hospital."

Why try to reason with her? People who believed in God had one foot in the well of delusion to begin with. Wendell fired up the Dodge and put it in gear. "You need an asylum."

"Ha. You'd have to murder me to separate me from Heather, and I don't think you're a killer, Wendell. You know what else I think? You've done some wrong things in your own life, my friend."

She looked much too confident all of a sudden. She couldn't know much, only having snooped in his shed for a few minutes. But if she turned him in…

"What were you thinking, Siena? The FBI investigates kidnappings."

"This whole thing with the cops should never have happened. I wore a wig and fake glasses, and I got one of these plastic pouches on a strap." Siena pulled an ID tag on a cord out and waved it at him. "It's like the ones the nurses wear. I faked up this card with my picture on it and wore it backwards, like real nurses do, so no one could see it was phony."

"How would you explain to your friends and your husband or boyfriend when you showed up with this?" He gestured toward the baby.

"Heather isn't a "this," she's a tiny girl child. And I don't have a husband or a boyfriend. Everyone knew I was pregnant. Only my best friend knows about the miscarriage."

"Siena, it's a shame about your losses, but…" He reached out and came very close to touching her hand, then pulled away.

"It's God, Wendell; can't you see? God showed me to the nursery in Santa Fe, and He brought me to you." She smiled at him. "God knows that you'll find it in your heart to help me."

When she looked at him, he didn't turn away. "I might throw you out of my truck." As he said the words, he was swallowed into the depths of her brown eyes.

"You're too good a man for that, Wendell. And you have a secret too. You didn't deny it when I said you'd done something wrong. Instead, you scratched yourself all over, when I mentioned the cops. If you don't help me avoid them, I'll tell them everything I know about your cabin in the woods and your shed and the suspicious way you've been acting. And the explosion, Wendell—I'll tell them about that."

Wendell tromped the accelerator, turned the truck around and headed south.

Chapter 9

Heather had been difficult—first taking a pee, so Siena had had to change and clean and powder her, which had been a pain with the pickup truck bouncing the way it was. And then the little queen demanded to be fed. She'd already gone through a quart of formula; at that rate, Siena's two week supply would disappear in three days.

But now, all was forgiven; Heather slept between them in her baby seat/carrier. Siena held her tiny foot, as she took in the passing sage brush and pinion pines.

She realized she was enjoying Wendell's quiet company, even though he'd acted like he wanted to get rid of her before. He didn't look at her, just straight ahead, as they passed through a tiny town called San Francisco, heading for Amalia, New Mexico again.

The road turned to scrubby, gravelly dirt. The pickup's tires ground on, vibrating the cab, bouncing, kicking up a cloud of dust behind. Siena tickled Heather's tummy. The baby cooed and gurgled. "She loves me, Wendell."

"She's too young," Wendell said. "Even little kids don't love anyone but themselves."

"Did you hate your mom and dad?" she asked.

She saw the way he blinked and knew she'd hit a nerve.

"Not Dad," he said.

"What did your mother do to you?"

"Not me. She heckled Dad, trying to make him greedy, like she was, like the whole world is becoming." Wendell tugged at his beard.

"My Heather won't grow up that way," Siena said. "You must know some people who aren't greedy."

33

"The only honorable human is in prison." Wendell shot her a look and said, "Just let me drive, OK?"

"Roll up your window," Siena said. "Here comes another vehicle." She rolled hers up too, watching a dark green SUV speed the other way, churning up a dust cloud that enveloped them.

They traveled in silence, past Amalia and past Wendell's driveway, to the spot where her car had careened off the road. He stopped, and Siena felt the nerves tie up in her stomach. "You won't abandon us here?"

He shook his head. "This won't take long."

She watched, as Wendell strode into the woods and returned with a half dozen branches. He used them to scrub away the tire tracks from her Escort and his pickup, and Siena smiled. Wendell's secret was just as dangerous as hers.

———

By the time they reached Wendell's cabin, dusk was graying the sky. Siena felt a creepy sensation seep back into her gut. It wasn't the run-down cabin in this secluded pine forest, it was Wendell; his wild, lonely, mysterious presence had taken the place over. And these woods would be a whole different place after dark, full of bobcats and wolves lurking behind boulders.

"Wait in the truck." Wendell got out, took his keys and headed for the house.

Siena forced herself not to follow. She snugged the baby blanket around Heather, and they waited in the truck's cab for a long time.

Finally, Wendell came out, carrying a couple of cardboard boxes. He closed the cabin door and carried the cartons to the shed. When he emerged, she popped the truck door open, but he held up a palm like a cop halting traffic and returned to the cabin. "Not yet," was all he said.

Heather began to cry. Siena changed her shitty diaper and hummed, "Rock a bye baby…" But she really felt like screaming. She rolled down the window and tossed the soiled diaper onto the ground; that would fix the bastard. She closed the window as fast as she could.

Now she could only see the outlines of the nearest trees, and who knew what was hiding behind them—friggin' grizzly bears... Goddamned wolves?

Siena rolled down the window and shouted, "Wendell, my baby's getting cold out here."

She opened the door and jumped out, about to take Heather with her, but that creepy feeling stopped her. "What's wrong with you?" she muttered to herself. "You've been alone with him for hours." But entering his cabin in the wilderness felt more personal and way more scary than riding in the pickup with him. And if he did something crazy, if Siena had to fight him or escape in a hurry, having a baby in tow could be fatal.

She kissed her finger tips and touched them to Heather's cheek. "Wait here, dear. Mommy will be right back."

Siena closed the truck door and ran toward the cabin, trying not to think of the wolves, focusing on the fact that she was the deter-mined one, not Wendell. She tramped across the porch, knocked and grabbed the door handle. The door wouldn't move. "Wendell, do you hear me? I'll start cursing, if you don't let me in."

She heard footsteps inside. A bolt clunked, and the door eased open. Wendell stood to one side, and she stepped past him into a dimly-lit pine-paneled room with a drab brown couch and worn armchair in the center. Bookcases, full of thick volumes, stood to her right. A closed door and a compact kitchen took up the far end of the room—a sink, two-burner gas stove and a plain white refrigerator. To the left, she saw a desk surrounded by racks of what looked like a half dozen amplifiers and a computer with one humungous mother of a screen.

"Close the door," she said and heard the panic in her own voice. He did as she asked, and she took several deep breaths before looking at him.

"I straightened the place up for you." Wendell looked down at the floor, as he spoke. "And put clean sheets on the bed."

And hid some incriminating stuff in the shed, she thought. *Dynamite? Drug making gear? The head of his last victim? Would a serial killer make up the bed?*

"Great," she said. "Now you and I are going out to rescue my baby."

———

In Wendell's bedroom, Siena laid Heather on a nest of blankets inside a cardboard box. She set the box on the wooden floor near the bed and watched her baby nestle in and fall asleep. On the side of the box she read, *Driver's Side Airbag, model G-524186 GMC Yukon Series 2007, 2008.* Funny, Wendell's truck wasn't a GMC, and it was older than 2007.

She walked to the door, opened it and saw him sitting in his brown stuffed armchair. A book lay on his lap, but he wasn't reading. He was shaking his head and muttering to himself.

She moved closer. "Wendell, this is really nice of you—putting us up this way."

He gave her a quick glance and handed her a slip of paper.

I'll help you fix your car tomorrow, and then you'll have to leave.
You can never come back here.
You can never tell anyone about me.
Do you agree?

_____

Please sign here.

She tried to keep from grinning. He seemed so serious, like a pack leader, teaching a troop of boy scouts about some merit badge, but he wasn't teaching, not even talking.

He looked to the side, as he said, "You understand it's only for one night."

Siena strolled close, feeling her stomach tense. She stepped behind him, laid her hand on his shoulder for a second and then walked over and settled on the couch. He didn't try anything, didn't look like he had it in him, the way he sat hunch-shouldered. She felt both relieved and disappointed; he could have reached up and touched her hand to let her know he didn't hate having her here.

"Of course I want to leave tomorrow," she said. "But I just don't know if it's possible."

Still leaning forward, he glanced at her, his forehead wrinkled in a deep frown. "You saw my note. Will you sign it?"

"OK, but I'm not sure about my car, that's all."

He ceased fidgeting and stared at her. "If you stay here, you will get me killed."

That was weird. "I do plan to leave tomorrow, Wendell. It's just that, you said you wanted to help me, and…"

He stood and stepped close to her, sucking in breath between gritted teeth. Her pulse beat hard in her throat, as she balled up her fists to defend herself.

But he whirled and paced toward his desk. "My life isn't important to me, Siena, but it's important in the scheme of things." He turned back to her. "If you remain here, my work for mankind might be exposed and destroyed."

She felt almost sorry for this deluded man. What calling could be more important than caring for the tiny baby whose innocent heart beat in the next room?

Wendell plucked a pen from his desk and held it out to her. "I don't want to be part of your crime, but you've forced me. I will help you get far away, in your car or by some other means. Then you can never come back. Pledge to me that you won't tell anyone about me or my home."

She accepted it, laid the little note on the arm of the couch and signed it. "If you say so, Wendell; if you can help Heather and me leave safely, we'll go."

Chapter 10

Late that afternoon Special Agent David Webster drove the green Explorer into San Luis, Colorado, savoring the fact that Bates hadn't spoken for the last half hour.

"Hey, there's an ice cream parlor," Bates said. "What do you think... chief?"

Webster flinched at that smarmy, pathetic voice. But at least Bates hadn't called him "partner" or said "lookie." He weighed the time they'd waste eating ice cream against the thought of a cool, delicious sundae after the dusty drive. Why not wolf one down fast and get on with the case.

He pulled into a curbside parking space, and his cell phone rang. "I'll join you in a minute. Order me up a low-fat hot fudge on frozen yogurt." He shooed Bates out of the car and flipped the phone open, calling out just before the door slammed shut. "Hey, thanks, Bates."

After learning the latest news from Albuquerque, Webster entered the establishment. He spotted Bates sitting at one of several tables with two sundaes, in clear white bowls, and two cups of water set out in front of him. Behind him, a teenage boy in white apron stood behind a glass counter, waiting on a woman with three young kids.

Bates smiled at him. "Your sundae's on me, boss."

Webster strode past, saying, "You should have gotten them *to go*." He moved on to the counter and stepped behind it, ignoring the soda-jerk's surprised stare. Webster grabbed two cardboard sundae cups and long-handled plastic spoons. Back at the table, he dumped his sundae into one of the cups. "Get with it, Bates."

39

Webster marched out to the car, started the engine and downed a spoonful of cold fudge, as he waited for Bates—diet fudge, but better than nothing.

As Webster latched his seat belt, Bates got in. He pouched a cheek, his expression half angry and half goofy. "You could-a let me have a minute to enjoy this."

"The phone call was from Supervising Special Agent Ramirez. Melody Reeves took most of her money out of a bank here in San Luis two hours ago."

Bates looked down at his sundae then back at Webster. "You could've taken a few seconds to explain when you blew my one moment of peace in this long afternoon."

Webster wondered how a grown man could fail to realize that every day, and every minute of that day, was fucked up. But Bates wasn't Black. And as a younger man, Webster hadn't been so damned smart either. "I explain things when you need to know them. Like for example the fact that the suspect may have ditched her car and may be traveling with an accomplice. Some kids here in town claim to have seen a bearded man driving her in a red pickup. We're going to interview those kids, if that's OK with you."

Webster watched the other man's expression—curiosity beginning to supplant anger. "If she's got an accomplice, Bates, how does that affect your afternoon? I'll tell you how it feels to me. This case just changed from a crazy broad wanting a kid to a possible ransom situation. And that could seriously screw up this baby's chance of living."

———

After the interviews with the teenagers, Webster spent a few minutes outside the house with one of the local police. Together, they called the San Luis police chief and arranged to have a digital clip from the bank ATM emailed to Webster. The clip would show Melody Reeves withdrawing her money, along with the 15 minutes before and after. That evening in his hotel room, Webster would examine it for signs of her accomplice or either of the vehicles—Melody Reeves' Ford Escort or the red pickup.

He settled in the driver's seat of the Explorer. Bates dawdled on the porch, talking with one of the kids' parents. Was that what they taught in the Academy these days—nurturing relationships instead of rigorous investigation? Then it would be Webster's job to show him the real world.

He dialed up Supervisory Special Agent Ramirez back in Albuquerque.

The instant Webster identified himself, Ramirez' gravelly voice came back with, "I would have called you in another minute; we've got important news."

"*Not the baby.*" Webster's pulse pounded in his ears.

"No," Ramirez said. "The suspect's neighbor in Alamosa, a Millie Feingold, contacted the local P.D. Melody Reeves told this Feingold woman that she was heading to her apartment to pick up some belongings. She asked her neighbor to act as lookout."

"Thanks, Ramirez. I'm on it." Webster started the engine. "But I'll have to goose Bates. The dumbshit is chatting up the locals."

"Webster, I know you have issues in your private life, and I know this case brings up stuff for you. But remember what I told you; explain, don't lecture. Become a mentor to Bates, if you want that next raise."

Webster hung up and honked the horn. Bates shot him a glance, said something to the kid's parents and stepped off the porch.

A minute later, Bates slipped into the passenger seat and buckled up. "We should head back to New Mexico."

"We're going to Alamosa, Colorado."

Bates shook his head. "When we were driving this way from Amalia on that dirt road that you were griping about…"

"Don't waste my time, explaining some wild-ass theory."

"I saw a red pickup truck on that road," Bates said.

"Really? A red pickup in Colorado?"

Bates wagged a finger at Webster. "It was heading back toward New Mexico. I didn't get a great look at the driver with the reflection in the glass. But I think he had a beard, and the passenger was a young woman."

"Good work, Bates—a bearded man in Colorado. Remarkable. A pickup truck with a woman passenger. You don't hear about that every day."

He pulled out of the parking lot and headed north toward Alamosa. "You may not want to hear it, but I'm going to tell you why I'm trying to move this case fast and why it chafes me when you stand around yakking with deputies and witnesses for an extra 15 minutes." As he turned onto Colorado Highway 159 heading north for Fort Garland and Alamosa, Webster glanced at Bates, who was staring at the road ahead. "When I was a rookie 22 years ago, some stupid bastard kidnapped a two-year-old girl from its mother in a park in Chicago. An experienced agent and I interviewed the mother, who was sobbing and barely able to speak. I promised that we would return her child safe and sound. After we left, that other agent spent a half hour reaming my ass for guaranteeing what I might not be able to deliver. Then we followed a lead to the location where the perp was holding that girl, but we arrived twenty minutes after her throat had been slit. We could have been earlier, if I hadn't fucked up. The other agent was kind enough to go with me and to give that poor woman the news." Webster swallowed and took a breath. His voice came out with a slight tremor, "The newspapers called that little girl 'baby Chelsea.'"

"But you'd have arrived in time, if that older agent hadn't wasted time shouting at you," Bates said.

"You'll notice that I'm doing 90 on this skinny road, as I talk to you about the way you were dicking around with that family a few minutes ago. While you were so engaged, I got Ramirez on the line. He says that the suspect called a friend in Alamosa about gathering some shit from her apartment. Is that enough explanation for moving north in a hurry rather than following some random red truck back into New Mexico?"

Bates slouched in his seat. "I didn't know about that, so OK, we should go to Alamosa. But we need to put it in our report."

"What?"

"The truck I saw."

"You can write this one, Bates. Put in what you like."

"Webster."

"Yeah."

"You don't have to be so damned sarcastic."

Chapter 11

Light seeped in around the window shade. Siena heard Heather
sigh, and she smiled at the thought, *a brand new day with my darling.*

Heather had roused her three times in the night, bawling—once
for a change and twice to be fed, but Siena had slept pretty well.
Yesterday had been so eventful; first the scary way she'd had to rescue
Heather from the hospital, then the accident, meeting Wendell and
overcoming his resistance—she'd been so exhausted that she even fell
back to sleep that one time after she'd heard wolves baying outside.
At first she'd been frightened, but then she told herself that Wendell
would protect them.

She jumped out of bed and knelt beside the baby in her cardboard
box. "Do you need something, little girl?"

She picked Heather up, wanting to hug her hard but knowing
with a mother's natural gentleness how firm to be. She looked around
the room, seeing no pictures, no mirror, only a small chest with two
drawers and the doors to the living room and bathroom. She carried
Heather with her, as she went in and took a pee.

Next she'd have to deal with the strange, shaggy, secretive man. He
had stared at her with those stern blue eyes, telling her he was going to
dump her out of his pickup. But he hadn't. He had made her sign an
oath to leave today, which was totally impractical.

She set Heather in the box, opened the door to the living room
and gasped. The opening was blocked by horizontal bars. Her stomach
went hollow, as scenes from her crime shows flooded in—that crazy
perp on *Criminal Minds* who tortured a dozen victims, one at a time,
keeping them captive in a secret room. And the time on *CSI* when a
madman buried Nick in a grave with a camera recording his panicked

attempts to claw his way out. That one still gave her nightmares…. And the real scenes of Siena's father bloodying her mother's face before the asshole ran out on them.

Her heart was going nuts in her chest. But a second look told her; these weren't bars but a bookcase. She pushed, but it held firm. The bottom two shelves had books on them, and she saw that Wendell had shoved the sofa against it. She might be able to squeeze between the shelves …or get stuck trying. Or remove the books and try to shove the bookcase away. "*Wendell!*" she shouted.

She backed away to take a look. On the top shelf she spotted a bowl and a quart of milk. Standing on her tiptoes, she brought down the bowl, which was full of raisin bran, and there was a spoon sticking out of it. She retrieved the milk carton, and a sheet of paper fell from the shelf.

> *Have some breakfast, and wait in the bedroom.*
> *I'll be back soon.*
> W

Eyeing the cereal bowl, she wondered if he'd try to poison her using chemicals from out in the shed. She sniffed the cereal and detected no scent of almonds or rotten eggs. The milk carton was unopened, and she saw no puncture marks, where a needle could have inserted poison. She squeezed the bottle, turning it this way and that, but no milk spurted from unseen pricks.

Siena added milk to the raisin bran, sat on the bed and wolfed the cereal down. Then she thought about her demeaning situation. "*Wendell, you can't lock us up!*"

What if he was going for the cops? No way. It would destroy his "work for mankind," whatever bullshit that was about.

She moved to the doorway and pulled all the books from the bottom shelf onto the bedroom floor. On the cover of one, she noticed the picture of a smug-looking, middle aged man. The picture looked familiar, and the title read, *How Bernie Madoff Ripped off Wall Street.*

46

Siena had heard of Madoff, a real swindler who'd been in the news a couple of years back. She tossed that book toward the corner of the room and read other covers, titles with words like *Hedge Funds, Economic Crisis, Excessive Leverage.* Was Wendell some kind of failed economist who'd fled to the back woods?

 She snatched a piece of paper that had slipped partway out of one of the volumes and read the printing:

AVARICIOUS BROKERS
PONZI SCHEMES
UNSUSTAINABLE, PHONEY GAINS
REGULATORY INCOMPETENCE
GREED THAT KILLS THE GULLIBLE
GREED THAT KILLS DREAMS

Each line was written darker than the one before, and the paper was gouged at the bottom. What had led him to such anger? She picked up one of the books, opened the cover, turned it upside down, but no papers fell out. She tried the second and the third, but then she heard steps on the porch and a key in the lock. She took a deep breath and prepared to face him.

———

Wendell climbed out of his pickup and swiped dirt and leaf fragments off the truck seat with a hand. Of course the dirt had come off of him; his back would have been covered with it from lying on the ground.

Not wanting Siena to think of him as a slob, he dusted off the back of his trousers, and then took off the shirt and brushed the leaf scraps away. At the hose outlet, he rinsed his hands. Good enough.

When he unbolted the cabin door and swung it open, he heard her angry shout. "*Wendell, what the fuck are you pulling here?*" The swear word felt like a stomach punch, and he knew that was intentional. He looked at her, there behind the bookcase, hair mussed up, brown eyes bright with anger, wearing one of his tee shirts that clung to her chest. She was one enticing female.

"What are you running here, a jail? Get this bookcase out of my way."

Jail. The word sent a wave of panic through him. No wonder she was angry—angry and bra-less and good looking. She must have noticed the way he watched her, because she backed away from the doorway and disappeared into the bathroom.

"I only meant to keep you and the baby safe." He'd told himself that, but it couldn't be true, could it? So he'd just lied to her…. "I guess I really wanted to keep you away from my computer and… equipment." His voice trailed off, as he stepped forward and slid the couch back toward the center of the living room. What a wimp he was. She had invaded his space, and *he* was apologizing.

She emerged from the bathroom wearing the blue pants and pink top from the day before. "I'm not trying to snoop in your business, Wendell. I was looking at your books while you were gone. Are you a stock broker or some financial wonk?"

"I would never… They're parasites."

She knows, he thought. *She brought up brokers to upset me.*

"So, Wendell, what are you doing with a box from a GMC airbag?"

"You ask lots of questions for a person who wouldn't snoop."

Still picturing her in that tee shirt a few minutes ago, he felt a tingling in his scrotum and a yearning to walk over and hug this strange girl—a dangerous urge. Theodore's downfall had been letting other people know too much about him.

"Did you eat your cereal?" he asked.

She nodded.

"I used a hand saw to remove the branches from under your car, and I cleaned out the engine compartment."

The girl leaned against the bookcase and eyed him. "I guess that was nice of you, but why, Wendell?"

"The fuel line isn't ruptured, and the oil pan's intact. With a new fan belt and some distributor wires, I may be able to get it running. Then I'll winch it out of there."

Siena smirked. "What would you do then, use it for a paper weight?"

Wendell moved close, and the girl stepped back from the book-case. He pulled it away from the doorway, and she stepped over the books that lay on the floor and into the living room.

He'd been thinking that this starry-eyed, crazy girl wouldn't be practical enough to recognize her predicament. He would fix her car, and she'd drive away, taking sexual temptation, the stress of dealing with another person and the danger of capture with her.

"If I drive that car, I get arrested, Wendell, and then you're locked up too."

"Why get me in trouble? I'm trying to help you."

She sat on the arm of the couch. "It's not that uncomfortable here." She stretched, her breasts pressing the fabric of her blouse, and he could see from the protruding nipples that she wasn't wearing a bra. Wendell's penis began to harden. He stepped behind the book-case and picked up a handful of books.

"Wendell, I noticed a tub in your bathroom." She looked into his eyes.

He held her gaze for an instant. A lustful shiver tickled its way up his spine.

"I didn't want to mention this yesterday," she said. "But you need a bath. The back of your neck is grimy. Cleanliness, Wendell... cleanliness is very important around babies."

Her words didn't matter; it was the image of the two of them in the tub that held him speechless. She had to leave his cabin, go far away and forget about him, before he did something irrational.

"Oh, and, Wendell, later today, I'd like to borrow your truck and take Heather on a picnic."

———

As two pails of water heated on the stove, he filled a bowl with water and put a handful of cat food in a cup. He set the food and water outside the back door and watched as the stray calico cat he called "Feral" moved in for breakfast. Mumbling to himself, "She's crazy, and she's dangerous, and she'll get me killed," he hauled the pails of hot water to the bathroom and poured them into the tub. "And why am I following her orders to take this bath?" He added cold to reach the right temperature, stripped and settled in. Soaping up his hand, he stroked his penis, savoring the image of Siena leaning back on his couch. *Not too fast, take time to relish this.* He leaned back, just pressing his penis against his abdomen for a few minutes, imagining himself unbuttoning the blouse and discovering those breasts, tracing a fingertip around a nipple. He stroked again, paused just in time, waited a minute, savoring, imaging her kissing him. Touching himself again, wanting to halt. Too late. He sighed.

As he lathered his beard, he considered: Maybe he could convince her to have sex just once—this might be his only chance ever to experience it—and then be rid of her.

She'd been right about not using the Escort. So he'd teach her to hot-wire a car and change license plates. She'd need a fake ID, which was no problem. He'd drop her in California, where she'd blend in with all those other kooks. And he'd never hear from her again. But if he had sex with her, he wasn't sure he could cast her off like that.

Taking her to another state was one thing, but what about the state of her mind? This wild girl-woman possessed some sort of fierce primeval mothering instinct that he found fascinating. But she had no practical sense. The authorities would catch her and ask how she'd gotten to California, and she would say, "Wendell brought me. He's the one who made me this nice driver's license. Didn't he do a great job?"

Chapter 12

Before Wendell had gone for his bath, he'd set two more pails of water on the stove for Siena. While the water heated and Wendell soaked, she had a little time to look around.

She was beginning to think that this cabin might be a great place to spend a few weeks, until the FBI grew tired of hunting her. But Wendell was a strange guy—dangerous?—probably not. Still, for Heather's protection, she needed to find out more.

She turned down the burners under the water, checked to make sure that Heather was still sleeping in her box on the kitchen table and moved to the bedroom door. The faint sound of water running in the bathroom meant that Wendell hadn't begun his bath.

The top of his desk was bare but for a cylindrical pencil holder and a large computer monitor. Looking beneath the desk, she spotted the computer tower. She turned it on and then opened the central desk drawer, finding the usual stuff—trays of pencils, paper clips and rubber bands, a ruler, stamps and notepads.... She ripped off a sheet of notepaper, opened the top right-hand drawer and found two boxes. Inside one were checks with the image of a fawn and mother deer in one corner. They said, *Wendell Hawthorne, Box 112, Cimarron NM 87714-112.* On the notepaper she jotted down the name, address and account information.

She opened the other box—more checks but... "Now this is funny." The checks read, *Myles Kennedy, Box 591, Taos NM 87571-591.* She copied that down too.

If she could get on the Internet, she could search for those names and maybe learn something important about how safe she and Heather would be here.

She'd only been at this a few minutes, but she kept listening for any sound and wondering if Wendell liked to take a quickie bath or a long soak.

The computer screen showed the familiar set of icons on a blue background, but square in the middle was a box, *This Computer is Password Protected. Enter Password Here.* She tried *Wendell* as a password, then *Cimarron, Pine Tree* and *Hawthorne,* but none of them worked, and she was wasting time. To the left of the password box, she tried double-clicking the *Internet Explorer* icon. The words "Access Denied" popped up. Damn.

A nervous outbreak of goose bumps on the back of her neck was telling her to forget the computer and see what else she could find.

Her gaze flitted to a little red light on an electronic gadget on a rack to the left of the desk. She flicked on the switch. The computer monitor on the desk turned black, and she watched as it split into four squares. Images appeared—Wendell's shed, the driveway and the woods on either side, the pickup truck and a path through the forest.

On the electronic box, she pressed a rewind button. An arrow appeared at the bottom of the computer monitor. She pushed rewind 3 more times, and the pictures began to change fast. The sky grew darker, whizzing past sunrise into night in ten seconds, and a minute later it grew lighter. She saw movement by the pickup truck, hit the play button, and there she was on one corner of the screen, getting out of the pickup—that would be last night. She was heading straight toward the camera, as she approached the house.

No wonder that bastard had known what she'd taken from his shed. And what if he had a camera watching right now inside this room? She eyed the ceiling and swiveled the chair around—no camera in sight.

This man is seriously paranoid, she thought. *Gotta stop before he comes out.* She turned off the surveillance device, put the checks back in the drawer and listened.

The file drawer on the right looked interesting, but when she tugged the handle, it wouldn't budge. Where would he keep the key? She tried under the pencil box, beneath a tray of erasers and paper clips, and several other spots, no luck. Almost ready to give up, she felt the back of the desk and found it protruding from a notch.

As the file drawer rolled out, the faint noise of the rollers made her flinch. But this was so intriguing.

She heard the water boiling on the stove and rushed over to switch it off. Taking a quick glance to make sure Heather was OK, she returned to the cabinet. She saw file names— *The Atrocity, Compact explosives, Electronics suppliers, Financial Regulators, News Articles, Wrongdoers* and *Finances.*

Siena grabbed the first one, *Atrocity,* and found newspaper clippings, all dated 1989. A few were about a financial swindle, which seemed like a common theme with Wendell. And there was an obituary for a James Hawthorne. She skimmed the article and verified; the man had left behind a wife and a 20-year-old son named Wendell. The last article was titled, *Local Teacher Dies of Poisoning.* Wendell's dad had been a 48-year-old teacher, whose poisoning was deemed "accidental." "Huh," she murmured. "Wendell's a sensitive guy. His dad's death must have hurt him."

Maybe she shouldn't be snooping in his personal stuff, but she had a good reason. She reached in for another file, but then Heather began to screech, damn it!

She locked the drawer and replaced the key. At the bedroom door, she took a deep, calming breath and called out to him, "*My bath water's hot, Wendell, and I want a chance at that tub.*"

Glancing back at the living room, Siena saw the computer screen still alight. She rushed to turn it off. And then she headed to the kitchen table to attend her baby.

———

Wendell poured the pails of scalding water into the bathtub for Siena's bath. Passing through the bedroom with the empty buckets, he saw her standing near the dresser. She had her arms folded beneath her breasts, and the baby lay in its box on the floor just behind her. He walked out to the living room, and after he closed the bedroom door, he heard a scraping sound. She was propping the bed against the door for protection.

It struck him then; this girl, who seemed so brash, was afraid of him and scared for her baby. He felt hurt; he'd never harmed another person ... not purposely. But this desperation her presence triggered in him was new and scary.

He yearned to get out of the house and take one of his three hour walks but didn't dare. She was wild but not stupid. From something she'd seen while still confined to the bedroom, Siena had figured out that he hated financial manipulators and she'd taunted him about it. How much incriminating information did he still have lying around?

What had she been doing while he was taking his bath? He touched the top of the computer tower under the desk. It felt warm. No worry there; she wouldn't have gotten past his security and wouldn't have had time to figure out the surveillance system.

But he should have done a better job cleaning up last night, and he shouldn't have let himself enjoy the tub so much. He removed his checkbooks from the desk drawer and secured them in the file cabinet, adding the key to the ring in his pocket.

He fired up his computer, and went online. A series of headlines appeared on his homepage. The third one down told about the kidnapping of the infant, Shirley Cavendish, in New Mexico.

He opened the article. At the top right, he saw what looked like a driver's license picture of Siena, with the name Melody Reeves underneath. The picture bore some resemblance, but it captured none of the spark in those brown eyes.

The article described the kidnapping, the beige Escort and Melody Reeves' background. A little further down it mentioned that the suspect had been sighted in Cimarron, NM and was last seen in San Luis, CO. Wendell felt queasy, realizing that the direct route from Cimarron to San Luis ran past the end of his driveway.

In the fifth paragraph, he read, *Melody Reeves was last seen in the company of a middle-aged man, driving an older model red pickup truck. The FBI is searching for Ms. Reeves and the unidentified, dark-haired companion with a thick beard, whom they term a person of interest. The public is asked to report any persons or vehicles matching the above descriptions. Authorities believe that Ms. Reeves may be hiding somewhere in southern Colorado, but the search area includes New Mexico, Colorado, Arizona, and portions of Texas, Kansas, Nebraska, Oklahoma and Utah.*

Wendell realized that he was grinding his teeth and scratching his chest. Angry, vicious thoughts about Siena clawed their way through his mind.

His mission was slipping out of his hands. The crazy girl was taking over.

He took the scissors from the desk drawer and bolted from the cabin. Stopping on the front porch, he cut clumps off his beard and dropped them onto the floor. If they were looking for a bearded man, it wouldn't be him. He strode to the shed, unlocked it and went inside. *Keep your mind on the goal,* he told himself. *But don't lose track of your morals. Morals, which ones? Thou shalt not kill, or thou shalt save thy fellow men from their evil brethren?*

He opened a chest in the corner and reached in to touch them— thirteen little bombs, each half the size of a hand grenade, each with a radio-controlled triggering device. He had specific targets chosen for them, appropriate targets, targets that advanced the good.

It would be easy to install mechanical triggers in a few of them, place them in a box in his living room and leave the girl alone in there.

NO!!! He couldn't even kill the guilty ones; how could he do such a thing to her?

Chapter 13

Feeling less edgy after her bath, Siena rummaged through Wendell's bureau and came up with a worn denim shirt and put it on. She slipped on a pair of his boxer shorts, which drooped and were about to fall off. The only slacks that would fit were hers from the day before. She really needed to go shopping.

After pulling the bed away from the door, she set Heather in her box on top of the bed. Moving out into the main room, she found that Wendell was gone, so she switched on the computer and surveillance system. When it came up, she rewound to the point when Wendell had left the cabin. He'd paused on the porch, moving his hands near his face. But he was looking away from the camera; she couldn't tell what he was doing.

Then he'd marched to the shed and disappeared inside. She turned off the rewind feature and let the contraption run on current time to keep an eye on him. This surveillance thing was pretty neat.

Feeling behind the desk, she stopped cold. The key was gone. Had Wendell figured out what she'd done? The check books were missing too. He *was* trying to impede her investigation, but she was on Wendell's case now. She had to know if he was a danger to Heather.

Siena rummaged through the kitchen drawers, removing a paring knife and a carving blade. She stashed the larger weapon under one of the sofa cushions and kept the paring knife with her, as she turned to the two large bookcases on the wall opposite his desk—lots of volumes about computers and electronics. One bottom shelf contained titles like, *Killing Yourself—No Easy Way Out, Why Men Commit Suicide, Recognizing the Signs of Suicidal Thought, Cowards or Criminals—A Psycho-Legal Analysis of Suicide.*

She was beginning to feel that creepy, chilly sensation on the back of her neck. So she walked over to check the monitor—no action out there.

Back at the bookcase, she removed each of the suicide books, one at a time, held it by its spine and shook. No slips of paper fell out.

If Wendell was thinking about killing himself, it might not be such a bad thing, leaving Heather and her a ready-made sanctuary here in this pretty forest.

She carried *Why Men Commit Suicide* over to the desk and began paging through. She was about to check the surveillance monitor, when something caught her eye—Wendell's printing on the open page. The heading on the top of the page said, *Reasons for Suicide: Financial,* and Wendell had written, *DAD, YOU SHOULD HAVE TOLD ME ABOUT YOUR MONEY PROBLEMS.*

Dad. Siena thought back to Wendell's father's obituary. "Oh," she said. "Your dad killed himself, didn't he, Wendell? I'm sorry." She jumped at a sound—bawling from the bedroom. *Damn it.*

Trying not to be pissed off, Siena closed the book and put it away. *Count to ten,* she reminded herself.

By the time she reached Heather, Siena felt a little calmer. She picked the baby up and hugged her. "Little girl, couldn't you call me with a whimper instead of a shout?"

Heather was still screeching, giving Siena a headache. She laid the baby on a towel on the bed and removed her diaper. With baby wipes she cleaned Heather's girl parts, and the infant quieted. "I was enjoying learning about Uncle Wen-wen," she said. "But when you scream, he can hear you *all the way* out in his shed. Now he may come and ruin my fun."

She re-diapered Heather, and when she looked up, Wendell stood in the doorway, glowering.

Shit. What's he mad about now? Siena's skin turned clammy, and her heart hammered in her chest. "Wendell, you startled me." But even as a pulse of fear rushed up her spine, Siena was realizing that he'd hacked off most of his beard.

Wendell turned his head to the side, avoiding her eyes. He was biting his lip again. She saw a little blood oozing there. And he was scratching his stomach. The man was so nervous, and silly-looking, and the poor guy; his father had committed suicide.

"Wendell what did you do to your beard?"

"I'm getting rid of it."

The chin he'd been hiding was pale, but he had a strong, angular jaw line... and that tall, lean bod'. The thought that he must have cut it for her sent a hot, sexy sensation running through her. "Don't be mad at me, Wendell." She moved closer, seeing how comical he looked, coming close enough to imagine that she felt the heat of him, man warmth and also angry heat coming from the pit of his stomach. But he had no reason to be mad, and he looked *so* funny. She giggled, as she reached up and touched his cheek. "You did a crappy job here, Wendell. There's stubble everywhere and clumps of left-over beard. You didn't have to cut it off out on the porch. You could have waited to use the bathroom."

He stared at her, chewing at the inside of his cheek, and there were tears forming in his eyes. "You left my surveillance system on, so I already knew that you'd used it. Since you saw me cutting off my beard on the porch, you also know how to operate *replay*."

Why was he being so touchy about this? It was only a picture of his shed and some trees. But she wanted to change the subject. "This is so nice of you, taking a bath and removing your beard for me."

A crooked, disturbed half-grin crossed Wendell's lips, and he said, "While you were using my computer without permission, I don't suppose you hopped onto the Internet."

"Why, no, Wendell, I couldn't even if I wanted to."

"Come," he said. He turned his back and stalked toward the main room.

She lifted Heather from the bed and settled her in the box.

When she joined Wendell at the computer, he had a news article up on the screen with her crummy driver's license photo on it. "Rats," she said. "They could've found a better shot."

Wendell jabbed his finger at one part of the article. "They know about me now. They're seeking a bearded man with a red pickup."

"So now you understand *me* a little better, Wendell, the way I feel with the FBI hounding me. You see why I can't drive my Escort away from here, right?"

He wasn't quite looking at her, but from the side, she saw that pained, patient look on his face. Strange, the way he seemed to get really pissed off and then pulled himself back into this depressing shell.

"I didn't cut my beard for you, Siena. I did it because of this news story. But now I agree that you can't leave here today."

"Don't be upset, Wendell. Your truck is all dinged up anyway. Paint it another color. Paint it white, and everything will be fine."

"*After* I paint the truck, would it be acceptable to you, if I take you and Heather to California?"

He still looked annoyed, but this offer sounded cool. "I'll help you paint it, Wendell. I used to work in an auto-parts store. And later, will you stay with us when we get to California? At least until we find new friends." She put her hand on his shoulder and then slid it up and touched his cheek again. "Wendell, if we take a road trip like that, we'll be two fugitives, like Bonnie and Clyde. Have you seen that movie?"

With her hand on the side of Wendell's face, she felt his jaw working. He shoved his chair away from the desk and stood. She stumbled backwards to get out of the way, landing flat on her back on the couch.

Wendell clenched and unclenched his fists, glaring, not looking at all comical anymore— looking damned scary. "*You are a stupid girl*," he shouted. "*Everything you do is crazy, and you are ruining my plans.*"

He whirled, crawled under the desk and pulled something out of the back of the computer tower. He held the power cord for her to see and then he stormed out of the cabin.

Heather began screeching again. Siena sat back on the couch letting the shock waves from Wendell's tantrum pass over her. He had upset her, and he had meant to do it. He was probably just scared of the cops the way she had been yesterday. He couldn't have meant the mean things he'd said. And now that he'd walked out, she'd have a chance to look for more notes in the books about suicide.

Chapter 14

S pecial Agent John Motz in the Omaha FBI office had been the case officer for the HedgeBomber fiasco for the past nine months. The Unabomber wannabe had been named for his propensity for bombing hedge fund offices and other financial firms, but his most recent target had thrown the FBI for a loop.

Under immense pressure from Headquarters, Motz' boss, Special Agent in Charge (S.A.C.) Hiram Wong, gave Motz daily doses of meddling. Wong was Chinese-American, 48 years old, three years younger than Motz.

Motz liked Wong, but only in small doses.

Now Motz and Wong were welcoming a new agent to the office. The tall, young woman, Natalie Brown, had black hair that draped a third of the way down her back, black, sensuous eyebrows and a dimple to the left of her mouth when she smiled. She walked ahead of the two men, entering the conference room, wearing a charcoal grey suit that covered what Motz imagined to be a hot body. That was still more hope than certainty.

Motz watched her settle into a chair by the table.

Wong sat across from her and winked. "Feel free to remove your jacket, Agent Brown. You'll notice that Agent Motz didn't wear his."

Motz took the end seat. "S.A.C. Wong should give me credit for wearing this ugly tie, not chide me for leaving my jacket behind."

Natalie Brown flashing her radiant hazel eyes in a smile, then turned back to Wong. "I see that you boost morale with a little repartee, Special Agent Wong. That's admirable."

"And Agent Brown has a nose to match her moniker," Motz said.

"I think I'm going to like it here." Natalie Brown slipped off her jacket, and what Motz saw of her body confirmed his best imaginings.

"We're here to welcome you, Agent Brown," Wong said. "And to give you an orientation about cases you'll be working." He glanced at Motz. "Tell her about the HedgeBomber, and don't skimp on details."

"This is a top priority case," Motz said. "We're devoting lots of man hours, woman hours too. You'll find the details in these files." Motz slid three thick, expandable folders to the young woman. "As you may know, in addition to bombing financial institutions, the HedgeBomber sends letters to the fund managers calling them leaches and swindlers, and demanding that they repent and repay."

Natalie Brown opened one of the files and scanned the first page. "I've read about him, Agent Motz. His first dozen bombs were sent by mail. They were all less than 13 ounces, so he didn't have to enter a post office to mail them. But all they accomplished was to give each target a good scare and a face full of Styrofoam balls."

"It may sound like a joke," Wong said. "But he's escalating. And the news media treats him as a people's champion. We're under extreme pressure to find him."

The young woman fixed Motz with a steady stare. "And you think it's a man, rather than a woman, because…?"

"We're not discriminating against women, Agent Brown," Motz said. "Though my boss thinks that heterosexual, male Asians occupy the top rung of the evolutionary brain trust." Motz savored Wong's pained expression. "We've consulted profilers, but you'll read about that in these files. Let's move on to the next case."

Wong sat forward, leaning his elbows on the table. "I used to love this case, Agent Brown. The bomber is enigmatic with a touch of the bizarre. Unlike the Unabomber, he takes chances that seem crazy, which he is, of course."

Motz gave a theatrical sigh, knowing it would do no good. Wong glanced at Motz and continued. "Based on the type of perpetrators who do bombings, this one is likely male. He would have been in his late twenties or early thirties when he began the bombings ten years ago. He has been the subject of a financial swindle, or he feels that he has. Profilers believe that he is highly intelligent, but the financial loss set him back. Perhaps he was seeking an advanced degree but was unable to finish for lack of funds."

"That was the theory in the Unabomber case, wasn't it?" Natalie Brown shook her head. "But the theory proved wrong. Ted Kaczynski received a doctorate and held a teaching position at Berkeley before he, ah, lost control."

Motz stood. "You fill her in, Agent Wong, but leave me a little time later in the day to tell her the stuff she really needs to know. I'll be in my office when you finish. Great to meet you, Agent Brown."

On the way out, Motz paused in the doorway. "Save the gorilla story for me, will you Wong? It's my favorite."

———

When Motz returned from lunch, he found Agent Brown seated in the guest chair in his office reading through one of the case files.

Motz cleared his throat, and the young woman looked up. "I'm never going to run this place," he said. "Or any FBI office." He settled behind his cluttered desk. "I don't abide with bullshit or bureaucracy. Is it all right if I use in-house language like that?"

"Now that's a different term." She closed the file and set it on top of the other two and then shifted to face him straight on.

"It can be awkward with a new female agent," Motz said. "For example, if I call the bomber a *dumb fuck*, I wouldn't want to offend."

Her look was dead serious. "There's a line you can't cross, Agent Motz."

"Have I crossed it?"

She shook her head, her pretty hazel eyes focusing for a moment on the picture of Motz's wife, Sarah, and two daughters on the wall. "You can call the bomber any friggin' name you want; you just can't get personal with me." But the look in her eyes made him wonder.

"I took the Sexual Harassment class," he said. "Let me know if I go too far, and I'll back off. Did Wong tell you why the HedgeBomber case is handled out of Omaha, when bombs have been received all over the country?"

Natalie Brown slipped off her jacket and hung it on the back of her chair. "His first bombs were mailed from USPS boxes here in the City. Usually perpetrators begin close to home. Later, they disguise their home turf, in this case by sending bombs from other locations."

"They taught you well at the Academy, little grasshopper."

Natalie Brown shrugged. "I've heard that expression, and I guess it's an allusion to some old TV show. I don't get the joke."

"Don't worry," Motz said. "I won't try to explain it." He leaned forward. "Let's get to the important stuff. Did you figure out, from talking to Wong, why he said he *used* to love the HedgeBomber case?"

"Seems there's a lot of pressure to solve it all of a sudden. Didn't this nut bomb the Chairman of the Securities and Exchange Commission?"

"Wong didn't fill you in on that?"

"He was too busy explaining the gorilla case in devastating detail." Natalie Brown rolled her eyes.

Motz took a silver-and-black thermos from the top of one of the filing cabinets behind his desk and grabbed two mugs. "You want coffee, Agent Brown? They serve piss in the break room, so I bring my own." She nodded, and he said, "I hope you take it black."

She accepted the mug and sipped. "Tell me about the SEC bombing. Wong said he was leaving that for you."

"Good." Motz pushed papers aside, picked up a CD case and set it in the middle of his desk. "When you hear about this, you'll be *dazzled* by the *genius* of our quarry." Motz was hamming it up, enjoying Natalie Brown's smile and the way her eyes never left his. No woman had looked at him quite that way recently. "Not only that but the care he takes not to hurt anyone. We don't talk with the press about that, because they're already treating this HedgeBomber pile-of-turds as a hero."

He tapped the CD case, and it slid closer to Natalie Brown. She flinched, and sat back in her chair.

"Let's forget the Agent shit," he said. "I'll call you Brown. This little box with its CD weighs four ounces. Pack it with conventional explosives and it will run eight. Put two of them in a package to make a decent explosion, and you can't mail it without having your picture taken at the post office. So what does our clever SOB do? He sends four packages just before Christmas. One looks like a box holding a man's tie, another could contain a couple of CDs but still under 13 ounces, one that might be a bottle of cologne. The fourth box is the size of a book. The inner packages are gift wrapped."

Natalie Brown picked up the CD case and eyed it. "Why no news coverage of the SEC Chairman?"

"We're holding it back to avoid embarrassing the Agency and the Administration."

"I take it those were four bombs, but if the SEC Chairman opened one, the others would be wasted. And why would he accept the packages in the first place?"

"Didn't I mention the word *genius*? He sent the packages to the Chairman's house, where there's no real security. Each gift had a note from one of the Chairman's friends. Which means that the bomber is either a great detective, he knows the Chairman, or he hacked the guy's computer. The notes all said, 'Do not open until Christmas.' And they were forged well enough that no one suspected."

"In the box shaped like a book, our bomber placed a timing device and transmitter protected in a Styrofoam shell. Each of the other boxes held 11 ounces of concentrated explosive plus a miniature receiver and detonator. Did I mention that this guy is fucking smart? While the Chairman and his family slept upstairs, *b-b-boom*." Motz slapped the desk three times. "The bombs exploded simultaneously, set off by the timer in the fourth package." Motz savored Natalie Brown's intense gaze.

"They rocked the house, pulverizing the Christmas tree and sticking clumps of pine needles to the living room ceiling. The explosion embedded shrapnel in the sofa and chairs, not to mention destroying the gifts for the Chairman and his wife and their 8-year-old son, little Jimmie—computer fantasy game crap."

Natalie Brown covered her mouth with a hand as she laughed, her hazel eyes sparkling.

"Agent Brown, do you find humor in the destruction of America's most sacred symbol, the Christmas tree? Do you think little Jimmie found it funny, when his Christmas stocking was filled with the cinders of his ruined Nintendo?"

"You're right; it's not funny, but I like the way you tell stories, Motz. And this guy timed the bombs so that no one would be hurt?"

"Three AM Christmas morning." The story was winding down, but Motz didn't want to end it. "I have jockey shorts that weigh more than 13 ounces, Brown, and this bastard blew up a guy's living room with four boxes that small." He watched her eyes, as she chuckled. "It's nice to have a perp with a sense of humor," he said.

"But the SEC Chairman doesn't. Am I right?"

"The president's the guy we care about," Motz said. "He's on close terms with our Director. None of them was amused by the HedgeBomber's message either. Here." Motz took one of the files and thumbed through it. "*Merry Christmas, Mr. Chairman. Through your negligence, you have allowed manipulators to ruin Christmas for thousands of people. They have destroyed families and driven men to suicide. In the new year you might resolve to do your job and regulate the swindlers.* He signed it *Santa.*" Motz had dropped his volume, and Natalie Brown must have picked up on it. She stopped smiling.

Motz hated to do it, but it was time to show Natalie Brown that he was dead serious about the case. He pointed a finger at her. "This insane bomber could blow up buildings if he wanted to. He could kill people by the dozens. He's made fools of us, and we have to find him before he does it again."

———

At 5:30 that afternoon, Motz stopped by Natalie Brown's cubicle on his way out of the office. "Don't know about you, but I'm going home."

The young woman laid her hand on his forearm for an instant, beamed and said, "I'm glad to be working with you, Motz."

The touch surprised Motz and sent a shiver up his spine.

Chapter 15

Wendell parked his truck a few blocks from the All Mart store in Las Vegas, New Mexico. He touched his clean-shaven chin and sighed. He'd felt peculiar since hacking the beard off and even worse now that he'd shaved his face clean.

He examined himself now in the truck's rearview mirror, his upper lip way too long, his chin jutting like a gnarled stump.

The drive here had seemed interminable—almost three hours from home, far from his usual haunts. But in Las Vegas no one would recognize him.

As he walked to the All Mart, it was eating at him—the idea of Siena prowling through his things in the cabin. But he couldn't have taken her on this trip with the FBI and half the New Mexico citizenry looking for her; couldn't confine her in the bedroom behind his bookcase. She'd have destroyed the bookcase and half of his belongings.

Inside the store he bought four quarts of glossy black paint, primer, finishing sealer and mineral oil, masking tape, dense foam brushes and sand paper. With his purchases stowed on the passenger side floor of the truck, he headed for home.

It was absurd, but he regretted yelling at her, especially regretted calling her "stupid." That was a crude word, and inaccurate; she was insane, not stupid.

The more he thought about her, the more obvious it became; he could never allow Siena to leave his cabin and the pine forest surrounding it again.

His thoughts turned to the design of a tidy bomb package to kill her, and how to entice her to blow herself up with minimal damage. If he set it on the cabin porch and left her alone, she would open it. But he'd have to make sure that Siena left the baby inside. Later he could disguise himself—as he'd done sometimes before—obtain a throw-away cell phone, drop the baby at a church somewhere in Colorado and report the baby's location to a local newspaper.

His stomach churned. If he did this, would the act serve humanity? One baby kidnapper wiped off the planet? Was he less crazy than the girl for thinking of it?

He considered again the idea of dropping her in California with a firm admonition never to speak of him—ridiculous. Or he could let her stay with him for a while, until he conceived a better plan. The idea brought enticing images of her lounging on his couch, braless.

It took him several minutes to realize he was driving the wrong direction, south and west toward Santa Fe. And then he remembered Siena's demand that he buy lots of baby formula and diapers.

Feeling conspicuous in his red pickup, he exited and headed north. He turned off the highway back in Las Vegas and went to the Piggly Wiggly store. Inside, he gathered provisions for himself and the girl in a shopping cart and found the right aisle. Self-conscious and nervous, he dropped in packages of disposable diapers in the smallest size. He added a half dozen bottles of liquid infant formula like the ones Siena had used.

But maybe little Heather needed a different type of food; she'd been fussing and screeching, and often spit up on Siena after being fed. He spotted plastic tubs of powdered formula. The first one said *just add water, makes 168 ounces*. That sounded good, but there were lots of choices. He settled on one that said *Fussiness and Gas* in a little circle on the front.

Further along the aisle he spotted baby pajamas and picked up five identical pink sets. He rushed through checkout and fled for home.

———

Ever since Wendell had shown her that Internet news article about her and Heather, Siena had worried about their future. They were famous now, which meant they couldn't go anywhere. Wendell's place was ideal, a miraculous solution provided by God.

If they were staying long term, she had to cultivate a relationship with Wendell, and she had to know everything about him for her baby's safety.

The lock on Wendell's file cabinet was pretty cheap, but it took two hours, using straightened paper clips and the point of a pair of scissors, to crack it. She blamed her slow progress on Heather's constant interruptions, all those damned screaming fits.

Inside the file drawer, she saw his checkbooks, the same files she'd spotted on her first visit and behind them some sort of gadget and a box. Inside she found dozens of blank plastic rectangles the size of credit cards. *Make-an-ID* was stamped on the top of the gizmo. It was the size of a small toaster, with an electric cord coming out of one side. She unfastened a clip at the back and popped the machine open, seeing that there was a tray inside, sized to hold one of the cards. *More waffle iron than toaster*, she thought.

Confused, she checked out one of the file folders, which contained cellophane sheets with emblems on them. The first sheet had a dozen New Mexico state logos, like Indian paintings of a red sun, symbols she'd seen on the state's license plates. Flipping through, she found sheets of Texas longhorns and Oklahoma oil wells. And there was a whole sheet of photos of Wendell, on the same thin cellophane.

Makes his own IDs. No wonder he can have two checking accounts with different names. He could make an identity for me and a birth certificate for Heather.

She pondered that before moving to the next file with *Action* on the tab. Inside she found only one page that said:

Four pronged action plan

1. *Attack the swindlers-hedge fund managers. Intimidate them into ceasing their wrongdoing.*

69

2. *Convince newspapers to print the truth. Make bombings unique to capture media attention.*

3. *Coerce congressmen and regulators—Securities and Exchange Commission.*

4. *Force them to act through fear and public pressure.*

The next file said, *Sunny State Financial, Mobile Alabama.* The first page was a typed note that said:

To Sunny State Financial Employees-

The bombs are a warning, not meant to hurt you.

You are doing evil work. Some of you may be unaware, but none of you is innocent.

The amazing gains your company claims for its investments are unsustainable. Your CEO, Clyde Turnbill, and your CFO, Manny Jones, are bilking your investors. Their false investment statements lure the innocent, with promises of impossible gains. Their failure to achieve those investment returns will lead your clients to the poorhouse—or worse.

Repent, and give the sheep back their money.

"I don't get it," she murmured. "What's this crap about false investment claims and sheep of all things? And bombs—God damn, Wendell what are you going to do?" She thumbed through the file finding ten identical notes, each with a different name typed on top, including one for Clyde Turnbill and one for Manny Jones. And then she giggled and called out "B-a-a-a-a-h. B-a-a-a-a-h."

She wanted to open other files, but Heather was wiggling in her makeshift crib, the way she acted when she was pooping her diaper.

70

Siena felt exhausted and depressed all of a sudden. This motherhood business, the work and aggravation, was dragging her down.

After changing Heather's diaper, it took twenty minutes, using the paperclips and scissors, to re-lock the file drawer. Then she lifted Heather out of her box and carried her into the bedroom, to snuggle in for a nap.

——

The outside world was turning to dusk—Wendell's normal time for peace and contemplation. He reclined in the living room armchair, but how could he rest?

He was tempted to put his work on hold, deal with the setback and then resume. He chuckled; *setback* was such an inadequate word to describe an insane woman invading his space with a stolen infant and the FBI on her trail.

But he'd prepared so much—the bombs for one thing. And he'd hacked into Sunny State Financial's CEO and the office manager's email accounts, learning the office layout, copying an inventory of the staff's personal computers and discovering the building entry code— but the code was changed every two months or whenever an employee quit. Wendell needed to get on with this.

He heard a sound and looked up. Siena stood in the bedroom doorway wearing one of his long-sleeved denim shirts and those same light blue slacks from the first day. "Heather's asleep; she's such a good little girl." Siena settled on the couch. "It was really nice of you to buy the diapers and formula for her. I'll pay you back."

"You don't need to," he said, thinking that if she insisted, he would let her.

"Thanks. What do you do for entertainment around here, Wendell?"

"I read. I go on the Internet."

She leaned back on the couch. "You should have a television and DVD player. Sign up for satellite TV—there are some awesome crime shows—and you can order Netflix so movies are sent to us."

He flinched at her use of the word "us," but he was distracted by the way her breasts mounded beneath the fabric of the denim shirt. She glanced at him, raised her arms over her head and stretched. He forced himself to look down. "I'd rather educate myself."

The girl gestured toward the bookcases. "About Ponzi schemes and what's his name—Bernie Madoff? What's that about, Wendell?"

"Greed."

"Everyone's greedy," she said. "That's old news."

He stood, walked to the desk and turned back to look at her. She was smiling, not taking this seriously; not the least bit interested that greed destroyed families and men. He felt his gut seize up and blood rise into his face. "It's about cheating. About brokers selling expensive annuities to kids in their twenties. It's about using computers to cover up fraud rather than to benefit mankind." He saw Siena push herself back into the couch. "The perpetrators buy yachts and mansions in Switzerland while they ruin men's lives." Wendell realized he was shouting, and he stood over her with his fists balled up. He'd never confronted anyone this way, and the fear in Siena's eyes surprised him. He took a step back. "I'm sorry. I feel strongly about this. I wouldn't hurt you." *Except of course if I have to blow you up.*

After a moment she seemed to relax. "You're well intentioned, Wendell, but you need to get a life. Buy some movies for the DVD you're going to get and stop obsessing."

Wendell began scratching his thigh. What made him nervous now was the way she'd turned calm all of a sudden.

"Lighten up, Wendell. Tell me about that cat I saw you feeding."

"Her name is Feral."

"It's lonely here. Why not invite her in?"

"The cat snuck in one time and urinated on the arm chair."

"Oh." She paused and then gestured around the cabin with both hands. "How *do* you afford all of this? I mean what do you do for a living?"

"I work a couple of nights a week online."

"So you're a computer geek?"

There was no way he was going to explain that blue chip corporations hired the security firm he worked for to clean their executives' hard drives. They didn't want the executives to miss a moment of work, so Wendell did his job at night. For eight hours on Tuesday and Wednesday evenings, he took control of corporate computers to eliminate viruses and spy ware. And sometimes he did a little snooping too.

The baby began wailing in the other room, and Siena stood. "Come on, Wendell. Let's get our hands dirty."

———

The next morning, after feeding Heather, Siena found the cabin's main room empty. She set two pails of water on the stove to heat. Moving to the bedroom, she stripped, found a pair of cut-off jeans in the bottom of Wendell's dresser and slipped them on. They were way too big, and she held them up with one hand, as she walked into the living room. She bent to unplug the extension cord from the pole lamp by the couch, and the cutoffs slid to her ankles. She imagined Wendell entering and finding her bare-assed. The thought creeped her out and also sent an erotic tingle through her.

Back in the bedroom, she cinched the cutoffs with the cord and put on one of Wendell's undershirts and his denim shirt from the night before.

In the kitchen, she cleaned the accumulated dishes from yesterday, then washed her dirty clothes and underwear and draped them over the shower curtain rod in the bathroom. Next, she moved Heather in her box out to the front porch. She set the baby down and took a deep breath, feeling a warm, dry breeze on her face, catching the scent of pine trees. A grating sound off to the right made her turn, and she noticed the pickup sitting in the center of the driveway. The headlights and metal trim around them had been removed, the side trim too. The windows and bumpers had brown paper taped over them.

Wendell stood in the front of the truck bed wearing a long-sleeved blue checked shirt, with sweat darkening the back and under his arms.

Leaning over the truck's roof, his torso rocked side to side. She thought he looked powerful and sexy that way, and she felt a little giddy, realizing what he was doing. She walked to the side of the pickup, thinking that his new clean-shaven look was so hot. "Hey, Wendell, you're taking my suggestion. Painting it white?"

"Black." He didn't look at her.

She watched his body sway, as he worked. "White's cheerier or how about baby blue?"

"Too conspicuous."

"Wendell, if you've got more sand paper, I'll work on the fenders."

"It's in the truck bed." He nodded toward the back of the truck, still sanding the roof like some piston-driven machine.

As she retrieved sandpaper, Wendell stepped onto one of the truck's running boards, sanding the middle of the roof. He'd un-tucked his shirt from his jeans, but his whole back was soaked.

"Don't you have any short-sleeved shirts, Wendell?"

"I prefer long."

"You can take it off. Wear an undershirt or no shirt; I don't care." She watched as he stopped sanding, still leaning over the truck roof, gnawing his lower lip. "You're kind of a closed-up guy, aren't you?" she said.

He started work again. "I thought you were going to help."

It seemed weird the way Wendell went from looking like he was sweet on her to this brusque guy who pissed her off. But maybe he was angry that he had to do this paint job in the first place; that would make sense. "Sure." She picked up several sheets of sand paper. "I'll start with this coarser paper and follow with the fine grain."

Wendell gazed at her for a moment, and she thought he wore a subtle smile of appreciation. "Right."

"I know about sandpaper and tools and lots of stuff. Like, I know you need to get a clothes dryer and a TV."

He smiled, but didn't look at her, and Siena liked the way his mouth turned up at the corners.

After a few minutes of sanding the front fender, she felt clammy. She took off the denim shirt, carried it over to the porch and laid it over the railing. "Hi, baby Heather," she cooed, but Heather was asleep.

From the corner of her eye, she caught a movement and saw the calico cat, half way up a pine tree, stalking a squirrel.

As she returned in the tee shirt and shorts, she noticed that Wendell had stopped work to watch her. She pulled in her stomach and pressed her boobs forward, as she resumed work. "Farrell's over in the tree trying to catch some lunch." She pointed. "She's skinny. You should feed her better."

"I want her to hunt. She may not always have me to provide."

"Some excuse," she said under her breath. Wendell was so damned stingy. Not having a washer and dryer was one thing, but starving his cat was shameful.

Wendell moved around to the other running board and worked that side of the roof, but sometimes when she looked his way, she caught him watching.

Over the next hour, her arms grew tired. Red sanding grit coated her hands and clung to her damp tee shirt. Wendell was working the other side now, and they moved in tandem toward the back of the truck. Her legs were sore from squatting to sand along the bottom, but she couldn't quit like some wimp girl.

She paused near the back wheel. She couldn't see him, but she heard the scratch of his sand paper. "Wendell, I know I've caused some problems…. Do you hear me over there?"

"Yes."

"If the cops hadn't identified me in your red pickup, you wouldn't have to do all this work."

"Right."

"Wendell, look at me."

His face and shoulders appeared, his shirt red with grit.

"I just want to say I appreciate it, Wendell…. And I'm sorry."

He nodded.

"You're a pretty good guy," she said. "Anyone else would bitch at me… Oops. I didn't mean to curse…. It's not too late to paint it white, Wendell. Then you could thank me for improving its appearance."

He ducked his head and disappeared.

When she reached the tailgate, she sat on it.

Wendell finished his side a couple of minutes later. He mopped his brow with a gritty forearm, and she saw that he was using the arm to conceal the fact that he was staring at her chest. "I'll just do some quality control, and it'll be ready for the first coat of black paint."

"Quality control, my butt." She gestured toward her side of the truck. "Take a look at the great job I've done."

"We'll see." He turned on the spigot by the cabin and began hosing down the truck.

"Give me a soak, will you, Wendell. I'm all cruddy."

He shot a quick spray up to her face and then turned the hose on his own shirt, removing most of the red. "Feels good." He grinned and glanced at her body again.

"Go ahead, Wendell." She grasped the front of the shirt in both hands and pulled it away from her chest, so that the spray wouldn't sting her, as he soaked her from the top of her head to her sandals.

It felt cool and sexy-hot at the same time! And when she released the tee shirt and let it cling to her, his gaze wouldn't move away. His naked lust and the gorgeous blue of his eyes sent a thrill though her.

Looking down, she saw the perfect outline of her breasts, with the dark pink of her nipples and areolas showing through the white fabric. She smiled, as she turned and strode to the cabin.

Chapter 16

It was 4:00 AM, and Wendell was about to finish his night's tasks as a computer security consultant. He'd worked his way through a dozen personal computers at a firm called Johnson Home Constructors. The firm's server had been invaded by a virus, turning the company's PCs into self-destructive hulks.

One by one, from his computer in the cabin, Wendell had taken control of the tainted units, diagnosed the problems and resolved them. He also took the time to read a few emails between one staffer and a co-worker. They wrote about a hot investment that sounded so good it had to be some sort of scam. Wendell noted the name of the investment company for future investigation.

He logged off and went out to urinate among the pine trees. Back inside, he locked the front door, stripped to his underwear, and climbed between the sheets on his living room couch.

Almost asleep, he was startled by a screech—the baby crying in the bedroom.

His thoughts drifted back to the night before, when Siena had showed him how to change the infant's diaper. He hadn't intended to help, hadn't wanted to be any part of it. But her demands were hard to refuse, so he'd followed her into the bedroom. After Siena removed the dirty diaper, with the nauseating smell permeating the air, she laid the infant on a towel and said, "Take some baby-wipes and clean her up."

With light brown goop smeared on Heather's private parts, it was embarrassing and disgusting. But his heart wouldn't let him look away; she was tiny and innocent, and she needed his help. So he'd taken the wipes and cleaned her with more tenderness than he knew he possessed, and now, lying on the couch in the darkness, he still felt protective for the babe.

He heard a clunk and saw the bedroom door swing open. Siena stood there, silhouetted in dim light. She was wearing one of his tank top undershirts, and that seemed to be all. He felt a tickling in his genitals.

"Are you awake, Wendell?" she whispered. "Did you finish work?"

"Yes." The tickle was turning to a rising pulse, as he eyed her bare thighs, her bulging breasts and protruding nipples that pressed against the cloth. Under the long shirt, he couldn't tell if she wore underpants or not, but either way she looked great!

"Make room for me, will you?"

He turned onto his side, and she slid in front of him with just the sheet between. Wendell's erection bloomed like the time-lapse photo of a plant growing huge. He realized that it poked out the gap in his boxer shorts and wanted to reach down and tuck it back in, but she pressed her body against him, nestling her forehead into his chest.

"I want to thank you for everything, Wendell—the way you've sheltered us and fed us and provided for Heather with the diapers and all. And I feel safe here with you, even when I hear the wolves howl outside." She patted his cheek. "And you cleaned my little girl; I'll never forget that. You're a tender man."

He wrapped his arms around her, not listening as much as feeling—the firmness of her back, the warmth of her body against his. This moment was so unexpected, so intimate and exciting—her breasts pushing into his chest, his penis against her tummy. Exhaling a long breath, feeling light-headed. And then he took in what she'd said about being a tender man. He hugged her and ran his finger tips up her spine, feeling the bumps of her backbone, thinking this was the best moment of his life.

She pressed her lips hard into his neck for a kiss. "When you said you wanted me to stay here for a while, you made me very happy, Wendell, and I promise not to cause you any more trouble."

She took a deep breath, and he felt, with his hands and his chest, the way her body expanded. It was wondrous.

"I think you've had a difficult life, and if you'd like, you can talk to me about it." She waited for a moment and said, "I could enjoy staying in this cabin with you, but I can't be stuck with just books about electronics and Wall Street. Let me on the Internet for a little entertainment. Did you hear me, Wendell? You're not falling asleep?"

Not a chance of that. He slid a hand down to the base of her spine, moving to the curve of her buttocks, finding that she was wearing underpants, wondering if she would make him stop. "I hear," he said.

"And I can't have you thinking I'm easy. There's no sex tonight, understand?"

He stopped moving his hand, feeling uncomfortable about that word.

"If you're OK with it, I'll slip under the sheet. Are we clear on the part about no sex?"

He nodded.

She pushed back and looked at him. "Say it Wendell."

"I don't use that word."

"Jeez Louise. Can you say 'no intercourse,' Wendell?"

"No intercourse."

She stood, and he lifted the sheet. He wanted to cover himself up, but at the same time wanted her to see. It was such an amazing moment.

She did see; he could tell by the way she grinned. Then she turned her back to him, as she climbed in. "How's this?"

Disappointed that she'd turned away, but still wildly aroused, he wrapped his arms around her stomach, felt her hair against his chin, smelled the scent of soap and something he decided was the aroma of femininity. He'd never smelled this before but had dreamed it often.

———

Siena ran her fingers along Wendell's forearms, feeling their strength and hairiness, pressing them against her stomach, savoring the closeness.

This middle-of-the-night visit was going great; obviously he desired her, and as long as he did, he would want her and Heather to stay. Siena was here to work her way into his affections, but she was *loving* the feel of him and his erection against her back.

She'd been feeling lonely, thinking she might never be able to see Millie and the girls at the store again. But right now she felt whole somehow, whole and wanted... and provided for.

She took his right hand and laid it on her breast. He explored gently with his fingers, as his pecker pressed her lower back.

"Mmmm," he said.

So does he have the gonads to pull down my panties? She wondered. *If he tries, I'll have to shut him down.*

He was sliding his thing up and down her lower back, just a half an inch at a time, like he thought she wouldn't notice. It made her feel so hot. She took his fingers and pressed them into her nipple. "You can pinch, but be gentle," she said. He did, and she sighed.

Taking hold of his other hand, she guided it down and pressed it into her lower abdomen at the edge of her pubic hair. She wanted him to touch that other place, but women needed to hold something back.

Sliding her hand past his, she touched herself, and now she had his two hands and her one working, massaging, stroking. And his penis too. Her shirt had ridden up, and his bare little man was stroking against the skin of her back, and then she felt the sticky moisture, and he said, "Ooooooooo."

She smiled, as her own orgasm took her to that rapturous place. No matter that he was only hugging her now; she still felt his closeness, as she caressed her way to another arousal. She would have reached for his hand to press it into her, but his quiet snoring made it pointless.

———

In the morning, Wendell applied the first coat of black paint to his pickup. As he worked, he noticed Siena looking out the window from time to time, and his blood ran fast in his veins. If only he could know what she was thinking about him and their incredible night on the couch.

When he finished, he cleaned his hands and entered the cabin. He found Siena at the stove, humming. Moving closer, he saw that she was cooking hamburgers and beans. She smiled and said, "I've been waiting for you to finish work, so I can make lunch."

He slid an arm around her waist, amazed at his own brazenness.

She leaned back against him and rocked her head side to side. Ripples of happiness coursed through him.

"Wendell, will you do me a favor?" She turned and faced him, and Wendell wanted to give her whatever she desired.

"I like being with you," she said. "But I need entertainment. I need to know how my friends are doing.... I need the Internet." Her voice broke, and he saw moisture welling in her eyes.

"What can I..."

"If I could just go on Facebook, I could read the notes from my friends and play some games. I don't need much."

He didn't want to do this, but the tears were running down her cheeks, and he had great computer security. "I'll think about it."

"You're a dear." She smiled and patted his cheek, and her chest-nut-brown eyes intoxicated him. "Clean up, and hurry back. I'll pour coffee."

As they ate, he had trouble chewing, because he wanted her more than he'd ever wanted anything, and because he was about to do what he really shouldn't.

Afterwards, he copied his password circumvention programs from the PC onto a flash drive and deleted them from the PC. He erased the temporary files and cookies from his browser, and eliminated the password protection on the Internet browser. "You can go online now, but you'll have to follow some rules. If you communicate with anyone, you can't give out your location or my identity, and you mustn't try to change any Internet settings."

It would be impossible for her to cause a problem with his hacker countermeasures, the fictitious name on his accounts and the routing through that anonymous proxy server in Manila. Still he kept asking himself why was he doing this? The throbbing in his penis explained a lot.

"Another rule," he said. "Never open an email if you don't know the person sending it, and don't open an email attachment, no matter what."

"That's two," she said.

"They're important. Our safety depends on it."

"Wendell. I get it that you're nervous, but don't go overboard, OK."

He stood behind her and rested his hands on her shoulders. She opened Facebook, and Wendell saw that there was this area with her picture and her name, Melody Reeves, and the fact that she worked at an auto parts store in Alamosa, Colorado. On the screen, in the area which Siena called her "wall," there were pictures of a few other women, her "Friends," and notes from a couple of them about the weather and a restaurant that wasn't good and a book someone was reading, all trifling things. Wendell had heard of Facebook, but never been curious, and now he wondered why anyone would go there.

"Look over here, Wendell." She pointed to a box in the top right of the screen. "There are lots of people who want to be my Friends." She turned her head up and gave him a pleading look.

"How does that work?" he asked.

"I click here to say yes, and then they can write notes on my 'wall,' like these notes my other friends sent. Or they can send emails."

"So their information will appear on your 'wall,' which is at this Facebook site?" That seemed all right to Wendell, since the information would be in this Facebook server, not his computer. "Have you done enough for today?"

Siena clicked the *Accept New Friends* button. "Don't stop me, Wendell. I'm having fun." Her voice broke, and he couldn't stand that. "I'll read my emails and make some changes to my Facebook profile. I'd just have to click this button, and…"

"*Stop.*" Wendell grabbed her arm. "I can't let you do that." She looked up at him, and he saw a tear stream down her cheek. "You can send emails to your friends as long as you follow the rules, but I don't like the idea of changing your profile."

She pressed her lips together and turned to the computer without saying anything.

Wendell watched for a few minutes, and then he went outside and unscrewed the surveillance camera from under the porch roof. He brought it inside and fastened it to a ceiling beam.

Siena watched, as he focused the camera on the computer. "You're going to spy on me?"

"If the paint's dry on the truck, I'll go to town. Is there anything you need?"

"I'm short on clothing—size 12. And you don't have any snacks; some chips and candy wouldn't kill us. And, since you asked, a water heater would make your life way better. A microwave would really add."

He stopped in the doorway, turned and fixed her with a serious stare. "If you give out information about us to anyone, they'll track us down. If you open an email attachment, Heather will be taken away, and we'll both go to jail."

She gulped and turned back to the screen.

When he returned two hours later with a package of chocolate-marshmallow cookies, a bag of Fritos and another containing 20 little Milky Ways, Siena hugged him. Wendell felt himself growing hard again and smiling like a fool.

That night at 4:00 AM, when he finished his shift on the computer, he stayed awake for a long time wishing the baby would cry and wake her.

———

The clock said 4:15 AM. Siena lay awake, feeling deprived in every way. That day on the Internet, she'd felt the usual thrill opening Facebook. But because of Wendell's comment about losing her baby, she'd been afraid to write anything meaningful to her friends or to update her pathetic Facebook profile. She'd felt him standing behind her, as she began, wishing he would make her get up from the chair to kiss him. And if he had, she might have led him into bed. But instead he'd set up a damned spy camera and gone away.

In her emails, she'd found messages from Millie asking questions: *You've been gone for four days; where are you? I read that you were traveling with a guy in a red pickup truck. How did you meet him?*

She'd written Millie a generic note. With resentment churning her stomach, she'd turned to look up at the camera. "See, Wendell. I'm a friggin' good girl."

Soon dozens of notes appeared on her Facebook 'wall' from some of those new friends she'd accepted earlier. The first message said, *I see that you're the Melody Reeves who lives in Alamosa, Colorado. You're the pathetic baby-stealing bitch I've read about in the papers.* She started skimming through the other messages and saw that they were full of terms like *slut, baby stealer* and *monster.* They all wanted her to give Heather back. *God no!* But they didn't call her Heather. They called her *Baby Shirley* or *Shirley Cavendish,* or *that innocent babe.*

She stopped and looked up at the camera, feeling she needed Wendell's permission to even wipe them out. "Fuck it." She jammed the delete key over and over again.

Further down in the entries she found a cheery note from a guy named Cecil Bates. The picture attached to his message showed a pleasant-looking guy, thin with black hair and a warm smile, kind of sexy. He wrote that he was a reporter who wanted to do a story about her adventures, write it from her perspective, so it would be fair. Smiling to herself, she vowed to take Cecil Bates up on his offer one of these days.

Later in the afternoon Wendell had brought her candy, and she'd seen the way he looked at her; Wendell had expected her to put out for him. Hugging him, her head had filled up with pictures of the two of them lathering up in the bathtub. But after the prudish prick had kept her from having any real fun on the Internet, he didn't deserve any favors.

The thought of him exchanging Milky Way bars for sex brought her mother's damned voice into Siena's head. *Don't be a slut, Melody. If you give it away for free, what man will marry someone who looks like you?* There was some truth in it though; Siena was a woman now. Her baby needed a daddy and a mommy and a future. Her stomach turned over, remembering her last relationship with a man. *Brian the asshole,* she'd called him, but which one of them had been the jerk? If Siena hadn't gotten carried away by the feel of his fine, long ribs, as she ran her finger tips over them, their one night stand might have turned into something greater than her second miscarriage.

For the next few days she'd hold back her passion. She would hum while she cooked for him, and in her head the tune would have the lyrics, *Siena and Wendell are Sweethearts*. Every day she'd hug him, so he'd get a hard-on like he had this afternoon, and in the end he'd want her all the more, want to shelter Siena and her baby from the cops.

Maybe Mom would be proud after all; her daughter was *growing up*, putting on what the old bitch called *feminine wiles*.

Chapter 17

Each day Wendell felt a tinge of excitement when Siena came to help him sanding and painting the truck. As the cool morning turned to warm midday, he waited for her to remove her long sleeved shirt. But each time she took it off, she revealed a chest covered by one of his tee shirts, with a bra beneath.

In the afternoons, she made him lunch, hugged him and kissed his cheek. She looked deep into his eyes for long moments and then turned to the computer, searching the Internet for who-knew-what, while he sulked out to the shed to work on his project.

For safety reasons, he modified his plans for the next mission. He reduced the size of his smaller, radio-activated bombs and tested them out in the woods. Next, he modified the timer-controller to trigger two sets of explosions and built two larger bombs.

As he worked, he fretted; what had he done to offend her? To make it up to her, whatever *it* was, he went out of his way to help with the baby—changing diapers, warming the formula before she fed the infant, even feeding Heather himself. He was growing to *love* the baby—if that was the word for it—but holding her in his arms, so fragile and exposed, terrified him.

When the third coat of paint was dry on the truck, he applied fast-drying sealer. After lunch, he made the two-hour drive to Taos. He stopped at an ATM for cash and went to a clothing shop off the main square, where a blond, middle-aged sales woman helped him find three pairs of women's pants—peach, pink and pale green—size 12. Then she picked out three white blouses with embroidered flowers. He paid a little over $200 in cash and then drove to a hardware store and purchased a small propane water heater and the necessary pipe fixtures.

Back at the cabin, Siena gave him a long hug and kisses on his cheek and neck, but none on the lips. As she ran her fingers up and down his chest, she thanked him for taking her and her baby in and for letting her use the Internet, so she wouldn't be so lonely and bored.

But that night she didn't come to him on the couch.

In the morning, she wore the new green pants and white blouse. Even with her hair knotted back, he thought she looked really fine. She made him scrambled eggs and sausage, and as they sat eating, he told her, "I'm leaving for a week on a project."

"Oh." He noticed the way Siena's mouth stayed open after the exclamation. A little chunk of egg dropped out, landing on her arm. She brushed it onto the floor. "Do you have to?"

She looked down at the table for a moment, and then she straightened in her chair and eyed him. "I mean Heather and I don't have enough food. And the water heater, you're not going to leave without installing it, are you Wendell?"

———

As Wendell crossed the state line from New Mexico into Texas on U.S. 87, he glanced over his shoulder at the locked metal box secured in the bed of the pickup. He resisted the impulse to stop and check the bombs; they were well packed and safe, the fuse mechanisms removed and wrapped in burlap. The control module lay under his seat along with the messages he'd prepared for the employees of Sunny State Financial.

Turning back to the road, the pickup's shiny, black hood caught his eye. His chest filled with warmth, remembering the way he and Siena had painted it, the look of her that one day with her tee shirt and no bra.

Siena—he couldn't think of her without feeling a tingle of lust or without worrying. Had he left her enough food and baby supplies?

After seeing how happy it had made her to use Facebook for the last several days, he'd given in and told her she could go online while he was away. He'd emphasized the importance of leaving the browser settings alone, and he'd lectured about not opening email attachments. Then all last night, he'd worried about what mischief that woman could cause in a week.

...He'd been thinking of her as a *woman* since that magnificent night on the couch. Maybe, she'd retreated from intimacy because he'd ejaculated on her back.

Just before dawn this morning, as he was preparing to leave, Wendell had taken the computer power cord. It had been the wise thing and easy, because Siena, asleep, had been unable to protest or cry or spit in his eye.

How angry would she be when she discovered his duplicity? Furious enough to take off and leave him?

Don't think about her. Focus on the mission. Go over the details.

First his justification: Sunny State Financial Mutual Trust had opened in the summer of 2008 and had made money that year, the beginning of the market crash—nearly impossible. The manager claimed that he'd picked the five best stocks of the last quarter and *only* those stocks. Money had poured into the fund all through 2009, and it had beaten the market again in each quarter. Wendell had read the stock-picking discussion in the fund prospectus online—a Byzantine labyrinth of deceit and subterfuge. The fund was taking in money, with almost no one cashing out. They could pay off old investors with the new ones' money—a classic Ponzi scheme.

He gritted his teeth and dug his fingernails into his thigh. A fund like this had snared Wendell's father in its fraudulent web and ripped his heart out. *Don't think about Dad. Focus.*

The timing: If he blew up Sunny State Financial's computers at night, he could be in and out and risk much less. But the impact would be less too. The FBI—and the government of the United States—would see Wendell as benign, unless he appeared to endanger the workers.

He had hacked into the office manager's emails again this morning. Their staff meeting was on for 3:30 PM, after the market close on

Friday, three days away. The meeting summons said *all staff manda-tory*. Since the employees would be just down the hall when everything blew, the threat would be tangible and horrifying. They couldn't turn their backs on his message; once the deception was revealed, they'd make the company abandon its fraud.

And safety: All the firm's employees would be in a meeting when their computers blew up, using small charges. To protect anyone who might be in the room housing the computer server, Wendell's tim-ing mechanism would detonate a warning blast 20 seconds before the large explosion—time for people to flee.

He'd revised and re-planned all of this dozens of times in his head. No one could possibly get hurt, but everyone, including the Government, would see Wendell as threatening. Why mull this over and over when it only made him crazy?

———

Lying in bed, Siena heard the thump of the front door and the sound of the truck driving off. She tried to fall back asleep, but she felt so abandoned, and she blamed herself. The last few days, she'd seen the puppy-dog look he wore each time she hugged him but didn't go any further; his lustful glances, when he thought she wasn't looking.

If she had given herself to Wendell, he would have stayed. But she'd been mad about his rules and then angry that he hadn't bought her a TV or a microwave, and she'd been listening to her mother inside her head. And now he'd left her, maybe for good. How would she support and protect Heather? How had she become so dependent on him in just over a week?

The baby began bawling. Siena got up, marched into the kitchen and set the bottle with formula into a pot of warm water, thinking that maybe Wendell was right that everyone in this world was selfish; look at how they started out.

She needed to go on the Internet to cheer herself up.

She noticed a piece of paper on the desk, as she reached to turn on the computer. When she pushed the button, the little green light didn't flash. No words appeared on the screen, not even a flicker.

She glanced at the note; *I'm sorry, Siena. I meant to let you use the Internet. I truly did, but it's just too dangerous. Please understand.*

Her stomach turned over, as she crawled beneath the desk and looked at the back of the computer tower. The power cord was gone. "*God damn it, Wendell,*" she screamed. "*How do you expect me to live?*"

Heather was still screeching. Siena shoved the computer tower, and it fell on its side with a clunk. She balled up her fists, charging toward the bedroom. She was righteously pissed at Wendell, needed to stop and take a breath, but she couldn't. On her way into the bedroom, she whacked the doorframe, stinging her fingers and sending a bolt of pain up her arm. "*Holy fucking shit.*"

She stopped and looked at her hand, as Heather wailed. "*Shut up.*"

The baby, the baby hadn't done anything. It was God-damned Wendell, the double-dealing, uncaring MAN.

Siena prepared the formula and then took care of her dear little girl. After Heather settled down, she returned to the kitchen, spotted the cat food bowl and filled it. She opened the back door and found Farrell sitting on her haunches, waiting. "Come on, girl." Siena set the bowl down. The cat slinked forward and sniffed the food. "What was Wendell thinking calling you Farrell? You need a feminine name like Jill or Amber." The cat nibbled.

Siena backed away, leaving Jill to her meal. "After you eat, take a pee on Wendell's precious books."

Under the sink, she grabbed a screw driver, jackknife and pliers from Wendell's stash. Using a kitchen chair and the screwdriver, she climbed up and removed the goddamned spy camera. She set it outside on the porch railing, aimed at the driveway and then moved inside and removed the extension cord from the lamp by the couch. Kneeling by the desk, she set the computer tower upright and examined the back.

She stripped the end of the cord with the jackknife, took two paper clips from the desk drawer, wrapped the wire ends around them. Using the pliers, she shoved the clips into the power slots on the computer. Holding her breath she plugged the cord into the wall socket, waiting for sparks to fly... but they didn't. Siena switched on the computer.

Who did Wendell think he was dealing with, some helpless female who couldn't strip a wire?

The cat rubbed against her legs, as Siena opened her Melody Reeves Facebook page. She reread her boring old message about living in Alamosa and working in the auto parts store and knew she had to change it.

Siena's heart was pounding, because Wendell hadn't wanted her to mess with this. He'd especially wanted her to avoid telling anyone about him or about where she was. Damned bossy, uptight, dipshit *man*. She wrote about changing her name to Siena, and about her boyfriend, Wendell. ... And then she went back and deleted it all. This business of being a fugitive sucked, but someday she'd be able to share her exciting story with the world.

She began typing again:

News flash from Melody!!!

God has given me a wonderful baby, Little Miss Heather. She weighs 7 pounds 9 ounces and is 19 inches long, and she has the most gorgeous blue eyes.

Like most new mothers I have to tell you that this was the most difficult thing I've ever done, bringing her into my world. But it's so worth it. When she looks up into my face with all that love, I just want to cry for joy.

If you're reading this and thinking of having a baby, no matter what obstacles you face, just do it. Do it now.

I'll have more news soon, lots of it.

Think good thoughts, and don't believe what they're saying about me.

Until I write again, thanks for being my Facebook friend.

She made the changes and saw that there were scads more people wanting to be her friends. Smiling, she clicked *yes* to all of them and moved on to her emails. Millie's note asked the same old questions about where she was and about the man in the red pickup. Siena bit her lip and resisted the urge to answer. Instead she typed, *Hi, Millie. No time to write. Check my Facebook page for the latest.*

She had an email from her mother too, which she canned without reading, and one whose subject read: *Melody, please contact the FBI*. The message asked her to get in touch with the FBI in Albuquerque so that the baby could be returned to her mother. It was signed Special Agent David Webster. The SOB.

She was tempted to smash the computer screen, but then she came to a message with the subject, *I want to tell the truth about you*. It was from that same reporter, Cecil Bates, who'd written before. He was asking about the bearded driver in the pickup truck. *How did you two get together? Is it true love? I think there may be a story in this.*

Siena wondered about the way Millie's questions sounded like the questions from Special Agent David Webster and this reporter. Damn it; could she trust any of them?

———

Wendell passed a sign, *Dallas 200 miles*. Thinking.

The mission was vital. Sunny State was stealing money and cheating people out of their lives. The bombing would expose the fraud, force the firm to go out of business and return what was left of the investors' money. Hundreds of people would be spared financial ruin.

Like someone should have rescued Dad … Wendell's vision clouded up, and he slowed the truck. "Dad," he said, feeling the tears flow. "We could have worked it out."

If Wendell saved one kid's father from being swindled, the father would have no reason to kill himself—instead, he could support his son and help him fulfill his dreams.

Wendell drove on for miles with tears running down his cheeks, remembering the way his father used to congratulate him when he figured out a difficult calculus problem or got an A in quantum physics. He'd bought Wendell his first car, after he'd won top prize at the Science Competition his senior year in high school.

He laughed at the thought; *my latest science project is a box of bombs with synchronistic radio-activated fuses.*

Taking a deep breath, he drank from his cup of water and focused on the road. *Think of something happy.* 4:00 AM with Siena, touching her body, experiencing the best moment of his life. And he'd been thinking about blowing her up. He could never do that now, never could have.

Chapter 18

Agent John Motz liked the way Natalie Brown watched him. Sitting in the chair on the other side of his desk, she sipped from her Starbucks cup, and her hazel eyes never left his. When she set the cup down, her lips curled in just the hint of a smile.

He'd only worked with her a few days, but along with the HedgeBomber case, they'd shared talks about their families and a little bit about feelings. He felt that he was getting to know her, and those eyes stayed with him, long after he'd left work each evening. She was just a flirtatious young female; he'd met lots of those. But it felt pretty damned good to be revved up this way for the first time in years.

Now he said, "In some ways our perp is like the Unabomber, Ted Kaczynski; in others they're opposites. Kaczynski made bombs out of wood and bailing wire. He hated technology, while our wacko worships it. Our guy uses high-tech timers and fuses. He hacks the companies' computers and uses the information to leave notes addressed to each employee, along with his bombs. The profilers say that he's electronically sophisticated, and he's showing off."

"Smart bastard," Natalie Brown said.

"Excellent use of language, Brown. I like to call our perp 'the Unbomber' because he never hurts anyone, except for that one mishap in the gorilla case. I wanted to release that name, 'Unbomber,' to the press. That might antagonize the perpetrator and get him to do something stupid."

"Special Agent Wong disagreed?" she asked.

"Yeah, the boss and the profilers nixed it." Motz realized that he was tapping his pen on his leg. He stopped and set it on the desk.

"Wong said that the guy is already taking chances like a one-legged tightrope walker with no net, so why bother."

"But Wong didn't say it that way, did he? He used ten sentences, including two dozen five-syllable words."

"Right, Brown. Would you say that to Wong's face?" Motz didn't wait for a reply. "Our profiler pointed out that infuriating the guy could cause him to blow someone's ass to hell."

Natalie Brown sipped again. "So even the FBI profiler swore like that?"

"That's the way I heard him."

She brushed her long black hair off her shoulder with a graceful flick of the hand. "Are you sure the bomber isn't trying to kill people, but he just screws up?"

"*That's* what I said we should tell the reporters."

Natalie Brown nodded. "Tell the papers that the guy doesn't have the gonads to go for it."

"Now you're talking, but the word is balls." Motz grabbed his thermos of coffee and offered her some. She shook her head, and he continued, "But as I told you, Brown, this bomber is a fucking genius, which he has in common with Kaczynski. He could have maimed or killed the SEC Chairman on Christmas morning. So actually Wong and the profilers are right; better not to piss him off. And there's another factor, Brown; this guy's becoming some sort of Robin Hood to the public. There've been editorials extolling the bastard's virtues, and millions of Tweets or Twitters or whatever they call them from his fans. FBI headquarters *hates* his popularity, and if we called him 'Unbomber,' we'd point up his non-violence."

"So you don't really want to call him 'Unbomber,' Motz. You were playing with my head."

"Are you ready for your assignment?"

Natalie Brown sat up straight in her chair, her silky white blouse following the contours of her breasts. Motz figured she knew just how hot that pose was.

He turned to his computer and opened an email. "I've received an updated inventory of the miniature timers and electronic communications he used in the Christmas bombing."

Natalie Brown stood, stepped beside Motz and looked at the monitor, as Motz said, "I'd like you to check for buyers in the Omaha area."

The young woman laid a hand on his shoulder. "That won't help if he stole them."

He ignored her touch. "So you'll check to see if any of these things were ripped off. And this guy moves around; he could have purchased or stolen them anywhere. Cross reference against our profile. This crap-head may have been a graduate student in electronics or computer science, maybe someone who dropped out of school ten to fifteen years ago.

"And we need to think about skin heads, gun nuts and other pissed off types. Fire bugs too. You, Agent Brown, will analyze everything your nimble brain can imagine against the purchasers of these little electronic goodies that blew up the SEC Chairman's Christmas tree and sent little Jimmie's gifts to Timbuktu."

"Is that all?" Natalie Brown stepped away, and Motz admired her calves as she walked to the door.

He cleared his throat, and she turned back. "Another angle, Brown—since our HedgeBomber is so sophisticated, he could have bought these items and then hacked into the supplier's computer to delete the record. Check that out too, will you?"

Natalie Brown raised a thin hand and wagged a finger at Motz. "You said he could have been swindled by a hedge fund or some other financial deal."

"Yeah, we've all been screwed over."

"I'll search for clients who lost their life savings back in those days."

"I like the way you think, Brown."

Chapter 19

That night, after a thirteen hour drive, Wendell slept in the cab of his pickup behind a deserted garage near Shreveport, Louisiana. In the morning, at a truck stop on the highway, he shaved in the men's room and devoured breakfast—bacon and eggs, over hard. Several miles down the road, he took an exit marked *Crowley Lake* and followed a two-lane road along a stream that snaked into the hills.

He pulled off at a turnout, retrieved his bag of supplies and hiked downhill to the stream. Kneeling by the running water, he dyed his hair gray, stuck on a gray false mustache and used a mirror to center it. He dabbed crème on his hair and combed it back.

Returning to the truck, he stripped off his shirt and Levis and donned chinos and a pink polo shirt with a little animal sewn to the breast. He added wire-rimmed glasses and brought out the mirror again. The man squinting at him in the glass possessed a far different character from Wendell Hawthorne of Cimarron, NM.

At the Crowley Lake County Park, he spotted a lone car with Florida plates near a campsite. He stopped and called out, but no one answered. With the Florida license plates in hand, he jumped back into his truck.

That afternoon, with the new plates installed, he parked behind a small hotel near Biloxi, Mississippi with free Internet access. Using a fake Florida driver's license, he checked in and paid cash for two nights.

In his room, Wendell hacked into the Sunny State Financial office manager's and CEO's emails, verifying that the staff meeting was still planned for Friday afternoon, two days away.

Tonight he would visit Sunny State to reconnoiter. Tomorrow night he'd plant the bombs, and Friday afternoon the main event would explode. Wearing plastic gloves, he remade the bed with linens he'd brought in his suitcase. He dozed off with his cheek resting on his own pillow case and his body wrapped in his own sheets—sheets and pillow case *and DNA* that he would take with him when he left the motel.

———

She'd lived through the night, but just barely. First there'd been Heather bawling, and later, she'd heard that sound outside, like something brushing against the cabin wall. It might have been a tree branch in the wind. *No*, she thought. *It's a wild animal… a bear; better a bear than a pack of wolves.* So she'd spent the night huddled under the blankets, cursing Wendell with strings of swear words to distract her from the danger.

And now, as morning light filled the bedroom, Siena wondered how long the son of a bitch would stay away.

She set Heather in her baby box on the kitchen table, filled the cat food bowl and set it on the floor near the stove. Opening the back door, she spotted the kitty sitting by a pine tree a few steps away. "Good morning, Jill. Come make yourself at home."

Jill sniffed the door jamb and then the food. She ate a little and began poking around the cabin, as Siena settled on the floor by the bookcase, pulling out volumes, searching for loose papers or writing on the pages.

Heather began bawling, but the selfish one could wait for a while. Siena found more notes scrawled in the margins of suicide books, but they were like the ones she'd seen the other day: *Dad, I still love you… They tortured you, Dad, with false promises… Mother's greed drove you.* Sure, blame it all on the woman. "Get over it, Wendell," she shouted. "That was 20 years ago."

There were books on communism too and *The Anarchist's Cookbook*. What a bunch of crap. Siena would go online and order some Danielle Steele novels, but this place in the sticks had no mail delivery.

Heather's crying turned to whimpers. Siena's gaze moved to the file cabinet she'd broken into the day before.

In the folder called, *Mistakes Theodore Made*, she found newspaper pieces about Ted Kaczynski, the friggin' Unabomber. *Wow!* From the articles, Siena re-discovered what she already knew; this Kaczynski guy had been seriously nuts, blowing up professors, an electronics store, airline executives, even trying to take down a plane.

Wendell's two-page list of Theodore's mistakes dragged on and on. Only one item stuck in her mind:

Huge error—resorting to murder—a moral lapse

The idea that Wendell was a bomber was nothing new, was it? Not after hearing explosions and finding the messages in his file to Sunny State Financial employees about bombs not meant to hurt them. And now that file was missing.

What a hoot! A bomber who opposed murder.

In his file called *Wrongdoers*, she found a hand-written list. There was Bernard Madoff's name, which had a line drawn through it with the word "prison." And several others she didn't know; two of those also crossed out—*Cosgrove Financial* with a note that said "Halloween bomb" and *Billings Real Estate Securities* with a printed "Blew up CEO's car." And there, halfway down was *Sunny State Financial* and the word "Next."

Amazing.

Siena straightened in her chair, her motherly instinct flashing red alert. She hadn't heard anything from Heather in a few minutes, which seemed strange; once she'd begun crying, the greedy girl never up and quit. Siena swiveled the chair and saw something like fuzz showing above the rim of the baby's box. *Orange and black fur.*

She gasped and jumped to her feet. Running toward the baby, all she could see was Jill in the box, and then as she came close, the baby's feet in her tiny little socks sticking out from under the animal. The words her mother had once said, *CATS ARE THE DEVIL—THEY SMOTHER BABIES*, ran over and over through Siena's head. As she arrived, the cat glanced up with a feline smile, and Siena screamed, *"JILL, GODDAMN IT."*

Siena grabbed the cat and heaved her toward the back door, picked up her baby and held her close, listening for breathing. All she could hear was her own pulse beating loud in her ears. She pressed her hands against Heather's back, trying to be gentle but firm enough to squeeze breath out of her. Once... twice... again. She laid her baby on the table and opened her mouth, preparing to breathe air into her. But the little mouth shot open and Heather screeched.

She unfastened her baby's diaper. "How could I have known the damned cat's a maniac? After I clean you up, I'll warm some formula and give you a nice snack."

Once Heather had gone back to sleep in her box, Siena walked outside. She spotted Jill climbing a pine tree and threw a rock at the damned little beast. Feeling better, she returned to work.

In Wendell's folder for *Financial*, she found bank account information for seven different accounts in four names, and there were two credit cards, one in Wendell's name and one for Myles Kennedy. Neither card had expired.

She logged onto the Internet, planning to visit her Facebook page, but instead she typed *Bombs, financial companies* in the search bar and hit enter. There were thousands of hits—like anything a person searched for—but among them she found a reference to *Billings Real Estate Securities*, which she'd seen on Wendell's list of *Wrongdoers*.

She clicked the link and read about a bomb blowing up a Mercedes owned by George Billings of Reno, Nevada, Chairman and CEO of Billings Real Estate Securities. The explosion occurred at night outside his home. Two days after the bombing, Billings received a letter calling him a swindler and demanding that he refund his investors' money.

That note, sent to a man on Wendell's list; it could only have come from him. The piece went on to quote FBI Special Agent John Motz, who worked out of the FBI's Omaha office.

"The FBI attributes the bombing to a man we call the HedgeBomber, because he's sent bombs to hedge funds and other financial enterprises."

When asked if the HedgeBomber's claims about Billings were true, Motz replied, "Billings Real Estate Securities is under investigation by another federal agency, but any allegations of fraud are premature." Pressed about whether the bombings had brought Billings to the government's attention, Motz conceded, "It's a new case; that's all I can say."

The FBI guy was trying hard not to answer, which told Siena that the feds had known nothing about Billings until the bombing set them on the swindler's tail. *You go, Wendell,* she thought.

From the kitchen table, she heard Heather crying again.

Siena waved an arm toward the baby. "Quiet, dear. Mommy's gotta think."

Intriguing as this information about Wendell might be, it wasn't good news. Siena had one set of feds chasing her—FBI guys from Albuquerque—and Wendell had another batch, but why in hell were Wendell's FBI guys from Omaha?

At the end of the article, the reporter asked if the HedgeBomber intentionally blew things up when no one was around.

"If you're asking whether the perpetrator has a gentle nature," Motz said with a grin, "I'm not authorized to answer."

"He does," Siena said to the computer. "Wendell's a peace-loving guy, and he doesn't live in friggin' Nebraska."

Heather was bawling, so Siena went to clean her little butt. When she returned to the computer, she typed *HedgeBomber* into Google and came up with lots of hits.

She smiled to herself, thinking that she was hanging out with this really famous guy.

One item on the screen caught her eye: *Man in Gorilla Suit Delivers Pizza Bomb in Chicago Suburb.*

Champaign, Illinois- The pizzas arrived on Halloween, so the fact that the delivery man wore a gorilla costume with a hairy black chest, full head mask and gorilla hands didn't worry the receptionist at Cosgrove Financial. Cindy Barnes laughed and thanked the beast.

Cosgrove Financial, another target on Wendell's list.

There were two pizza boxes, bound together with twine, which Ms. Barnes later realized was unusual. And she didn't think that anyone at the firm had ordered pizza. When she turned back to ask the gorilla if he'd delivered them to the wrong office, the ape had escaped.

But there was a note on the pizza box; "To Cosgrove Financial. Compliments of a satisfied client." Cindy Barnes took the boxes to the conference room and cut the twine.

The pizza boxes came, not with anchovies, not even with pizzas inside, but with a violent message. By cutting the string, Cindy Barnes set off an explosion that rocked the conference room with "a sound somewhere between a roar and a huge pop," according to witnesses from nearby offices.

The explosion catapulted Ms. Barnes against a wall, and she lost consciousness. When she came to, she was surrounded by co-workers, and the conference room was strewn with cardboard fragments, ragged pieces of white plastic sheeting and leaflets declaring that "Cosgrove Financial is stealing from its customers."

The FBI would not confirm, but there's speculation that this explosion is the work of the HedgeBomber. This notorious fugitive has mailed bombs to about 20 hedge fund executives in the past ten years, but he has never before delivered them in costume.

The plastic sheeting found at the scene was consistent with pieces of a vehicle air bag. "It's the craziest thing," an anonymous police source commented. "Like this nut job put his bomb inside the air bag to protect people from the explosion."

Three hours after the impact, Cindy Barnes lay in a bed at Community Hospital recovering from a concussion and a broken arm. When told the theory that the bomb had been set inside a vehicle air bag to protect her, Ms. Barnes nodded to the cast on her arm and said, "That sure worked out great."

Describing the bomber, she said, "He had nice blue eyes. My husband is six-two, and this monkey was taller." Then Ms. Barnes began to giggle.

"Holy shit, Wendell. You're a quirky guy," Siena said. "And a man of action." Not only that, he was clever enough to wear elevator shoes. Wendell was less than six feet tall, and Siena wondered if his ruse had fooled FBI Special Agent John Motz.

After feeding Heather, she read a follow-up article from three days later. Agent Motz confirmed that the HedgeBomber appeared to be involved in the "gorilla bombing" and that the bomber used a vehicle air bag, "apparently in a futile attempt to limit the explosive force." The article also noted that the HedgeBomber had sent an apology to Cindy Barnes, concluding with the words, *"I'm truly sorry, and I promise to be more careful next time."*

Motz was quoted as saying, "If he's so sorry, why not order her a bouquet or maybe send some mope in a monkey suit to sing an apology?"

Chapter 20

Agent David Webster stared at the picture on his desk—his daughter, Penny, in her Milwaukee High cheerleader's outfit. As he shifted his gaze to the picturesque block of adobe buildings outside the window, he vowed to call her and his son, Thomas, tonight.

His meeting with Baby Shirley's parents was fifteen minutes away, and he had nothing good to tell them. He'd looked up the statistics on the FBI network; the likelihood of recovering a kidnapped baby gone over two weeks was under 20%, the remaining 80% split between discovering her dead body and never recovering her at all. He wanted a drink. He wanted something positive to tell these parents.

Etched in his memory, haunting him every night, and especially vivid at this moment, was the memory of his first kidnapping victim's mother, 22 years ago. He'd watched the tears run down her torture-contorted face and heard her anguished wail, when they'd told her that "Baby Chelsea" had been murdered.

And, without some miracle, this kidnapping would have the same outcome. His *career*, if that was the proper name for it, would drag on until mandatory retirement at 57, and then obsolescence and nagging memories of failure.

He popped two antacids, as he walked down the hall to Cecil Bates' cubicle.

Bates looked up from his computer screen, and for once he didn't look smug.

"Got anything new?" Webster asked.

"Melody Reeves looked at her Facebook page again and erased the nasty comments people wrote about her. And she wrote another email to her friend, Millie Feingold, but she's not giving Feingold any info."

"The tech guys haven't…"

Bates shook his head. "It's that anonymous server in the Philippines. They say there's no way to link the contact back to her location."

"The damned FBI is supposed to have the best technology in the world."

Bates looked him in the eye and said, "The tech guys and I came up with something that might work. I'll send an email to Melody with an attachment containing a virus. It's not definite, but we think …" Bates looked down at his desk, his body language revealing his own doubts.

Calling her "Melody" pissed Webster off, but this was something. "Pump yourself up, Bates. You have to explain this to the parents, so it sounds like we high-tech FBI agents are doing more than jerking off." Webster motioned for Bates to get up. "And don't, under any circumstances, mention that red pickup truck you think you saw going south into New Mexico the day of the kidnapping."

Stopping by his office, Webster grabbed his charcoal grey suit jacket, and he slipped it on, as he led Bates to the conference room.

Inside they found Stan and Rosemary Cavendish—the thirty-year-old mother sitting at the table and her stout, hyperactive husband pacing along the back wall. The woman looked even more haggard than she had the last time Webster had met her, the bags under her eyes darker. She wore a stained yellow blouse, and her shoulder-length, dirty-blond hair looked oily.

She looked up at Webster with a sad smile and pushed her hair back from her face. "I know I'm a mess. I went through twelve hours of labor a few weeks ago, and this whole ordeal. It feels like I never got out of the delivery room."

Webster shook his head.

Bates said, "You look fine, Mrs. Cavendish. We understand."

Stan Cavendish's pacing came to a rigid halt, and he scrutinized the FBI agents. Webster noticed that, unlike his wife, Cavendish had spent time grooming; his short-clipped hair appeared clean, as did his white polo shirt.

Webster moved to the conference table, "As I told you on the phone, we've invited you for an update, Mr. and Mrs. Cavendish."

Webster gestured to a chair, but Mr. Cavendish ignored him. Webster remained standing.

"You have new leads?" Rosemary Cavendish asked.

Mr. Cavendish approached his wife from behind and put his hand on her shoulder.

"Nothing material," Webster said. "We told you at our last meeting about the alerts we sent out to FBI agents and police departments. We've given them full descriptions of the suspect, her possible accomplice and the vehicles. Every FBI agent in the country has a picture of the suspect. We've also spoken with all of Melody Reeves' relatives, friends and co-workers. The bearded man with the red pickup truck is not a known associate of hers. He may have been a stranger she met that day or..."

"Or what?" Mr. Cavendish interjected.

"It could be something more..." The word *sinister* came to mind, but Webster avoided it. "We're not sure, but we've found some positive information about the suspect; she's had two miscarriages, including a recent one."

Cavendish blew out a loud breath. "You want us to pity the bitch?"

"No," Webster said. "But think about it. If she's trying to replace a baby she's lost, she'll want to take care of your infant."

Shirley Cavendish smiled up at her husband. "That is good news, Stanley."

"Only if these guys find her."

"We haven't let up on this," Webster said. "In addition to the other measures, we have a new approach. As we explained before, the suspect is using a computer to access her Internet accounts."

"You said you'd trace her location through that computer," Cavendish said.

"Our lab has tried, but there's a complication. Agent Bates will explain."

Bates cleared his throat. "She's using an untraceable Internet account."

"Untraceable." Stan Cavendish's face was turning red, and Webster saw the muscles straining in his neck. "You've got to do better than that."

Bates put his hands on the back of a chair and leaned toward the couple. "It's called a proxy server, located in the Philippines. When users access it, the server doesn't retain information about their identities. We suspect that Melody Reeves' partner is knowledgeable about computers."

"Ain't the FBI friggin' knowledgeable?" Cavendish snapped.

"Don't blame them, Stanley," his wife said. "They're trying everything they know."

Bates took a breath. "The computer the suspect is using will have state-of-the-art virus protection, but the FBI technologists have created a new bug. We can plant this virus in a file and send the file attached to an email. If it works, the computer will send us back its user name and IP. We have to hope that her computer doesn't detect the virus." Bates held up a finger. "That's first, and we have a good chance there." He held up another finger. "We also have to trick this woman into opening the email and the attachment." Third finger.

"Why would this bitch open an email from the FBI?" Cavendish asked.

"We don't think that Ms. Reeves is a computer expert, like her accomplice," Bates said. "And she won't know it's from the FBI; she'll think it's from a reporter wanting to write about her."

Webster added, "Ms. Reeves is a needy woman. She goes to a website called Facebook, where lonely people go to pretend they have friends. There's no guarantee, but this has a chance."

"Ain't going to work. This young agent may not know it, but Agent Webster, you know that damned well."

Webster wanted to contradict him, but he was silenced by the memory of a similar meeting with baby Chelsea's parents, before her death.

Stan Cavendish tapped his wife on the arm. "Come on, Rosie, let's go home."

Rosemary Cavendish stood. "Do you have anything else to tell us, Agent Webster?"

Webster forced himself to speak calmly. "I can't tell you Mr. and Mrs. Cavendish how badly I want to solve this case."

Chapter 21

Around 1:30 AM, Wendell drove to the outskirts of Mobile where he picked out a dimly-lit commercial development. In the back lot of a termite control company, he found an unlocked pickup truck with the picture of a giant spider on the door. He spent a minute scanning the lot and adjacent buildings, as he put on plastic gloves. Then he climbed in and hotwired the truck. He drove to Sunny State Financial and parked a block away.

From everything he'd learned, the first security patrol would have come by around 1:00 AM, and they wouldn't return until about 3:00 AM. There were no surveillance cameras. But acquiring the vehicle had taken a while; it was already 2:15. As he approached the office on foot, he pulled on the Barak Obama mask he'd brought.

He punched in the entry key-code, entered and closed the door behind him. Taking out his mini flashlight, he ran the beam over the reception desk and spotted the alarm-deactivation keypad on the wall. His palms were sweaty as he stepped behind the desk and punched in the code. Entering a 5 instead of a 2, he hit *clear* and started over. He missed a second time; this was taking too long. Wendell took a breath and forced himself to slow down, finally getting it right.

His heart beat fast and hard, as he moved from office to office, peeking beneath each desk to check computer towers. He found the locked offices with placards that read: *CEO, Clyde Turnbill* and *CFO, Manny Jones* and the one that that said *Equipment.* The computer server would be in there. He took a deep breath and checked his watch—2:45 AM. The security patrol would drive through any minute, but before he left, Wendell took the time to murmur, "I'm not going to hurt any of you. I'll make sure of it."

Ripping off his mask as he ran, he jumped into the termite company's pickup. With the lights off he watched the security truck enter the parking lot at Sunny State and depart a few minutes later.

He had to control his nerves, but how could he not be terrified? Capture would not only end Wendell's mission. The FBI would find Siena. *She deserved to be caught, didn't she? Heather's real mother should have her infant.* Wendell knew this in his rational mind, but the rational was abandoning him. He realized that, more and more, he was looking forward to a homecoming and a long, voluptuous embrace with Siena...

In the early morning hours in his motel room, he fanaticized about far more than a hug.

———

Damn it. Why hadn't Wendell returned? Sure it had only been three days, but didn't he know she'd be lonely and Goddamned scared? Didn't he know she'd find out that he was the famous HedgeBomber and that his fame would make her horny as a rabbit?

Last night, she'd gone to bed comforting herself by imagining the welcome she'd give him, kissing him until their tongues got to really know each other, ripping off his shirt and caressing his chest, leading him to the bathtub and then to bed. She'd touched herself and felt tingly and warm and loved by him, until she remembered that he wasn't there.

Then, in the early morning hours, she'd woken to the sounds of wolves baying and pulled the blankets over her head. Despair had taken her, and, with it, came the certainty that he'd never come back. Who would protect them then from the beasts of this evil forest? How would she earn money to feed and care for her greedy little one? How could they get food and supplies? How, Goddamn it? How could she get the wolves out of her head?

When Heather began crying at sunrise, Siena cleaned her messy little tush and fed her formula, and then she went into the living room and switched on their computer.

She needed to communicate with another human, and she needed provisions.

Ignoring her craving for Facebook, Siena opened Google Earth. She typed in *Cimarron, NM* and hit *enter.* On the screen the earth began to rotate and zero in on the southwestern US. Then she saw the little berg of Cimarron, with US 64, the Kit Carson Highway, running west to east. Zooming out and shifting the map, she displayed the road from Cimarron to Amalia. Wendell's cabin would be somewhere along there. She looked at the sharpest turns where the road passed through the mountains and thought of the bend where she'd gone off the road.

Wendell's place was far from its nearest neighbor, on the right side, with two roofs that should be visible between the pine trees. Yes; that had to be it. She marked the spot, zoomed out and estimated the distance—about 35 miles from the junction with Route 64.

Next she Googled *Rural Food Delivery* and found a company that delivered to out-of-the-way places in New Mexico with a minimum order of $100. She pulled out Wendell's credit card and began filling her "cart" on the website—a few half gallons of chocolate almond mocha ice cream, two jars of hot fudge, bags of tortilla chips in assorted flavors, three jars of salsa, avocados, five frozen containers of Lobster Newberg and a few shrimp cocktails. She entered the credit card information and directions for delivery.

Having accomplished something to improve their lives, she moved on to other needs. On Facebook she got really pissed off as she read and deleted dozens of messages calling her *bitch* and *baby killer* and other crazy stuff.

She realized that Heather was screaming and wondered how long the noise had been going on. Figuring that the formula was warm enough at room temperature—she walked to the table and lifted the baby out of her box. "You're just a selfish girl." She felt Heather's warm, snuggly little bod' as the infant fed. And then she burped Heather and burped her some more and held her for a long time until the babe fell asleep.

Back at the computer, she began typing a message for her Facebook friends, *I can't believe that SOBs are judging me the way they are. All I've done is to love my baby like any other mom.* She paused, noticing the picture of the reporter, Cecil Bates. He had a trustworthy face, with dark features and a warm smile. So she typed, *All but Cecil Bates. Thank you Mr. Bates.* And she posted the note.

She went outside and followed a trail winding through the unspoiled forest, savoring the fresh, cool air. After a few minutes, she found a clearing with charred craters in the earth and nearby, a strange rig of some sort. She touched the blackened dirt in one of the craters and sniffed her fingers—an acrid, charred smell. "Bombs," she said. No surprise there.

She moved to the strange apparatus—four parallel wooden beams set on rocks. The beams were about as long as a car, with automobile bumpers fastened on front and back, like a pretend car without wheels that kids might play on. "Wendell, what the fuck is this?" She circled the pretend car, knelt and peered beneath. It made no sense to her, but she had a feeling that Wendell planned to bomb the shit out of this thing.

Returning to the cabin, on Facebook she found a new picture with Cecil Bates holding a little blond girl in his arms. The kid wore a pink jumpsuit, and she looked about six or seven. Next to the picture, was a note: *I wrote you a personal email. Go check it out.*

Siena went to her emails and found Cecil's note. *I sympathize with your situation. You're getting a raw deal, and I'd like to tell your true story. I hope you like this picture of me with my little girl, Penny. You're a single mom, and I'm a single dad. We should get to know each other.*

She wrote back, *Your little girl is pretty, and you sound nice. I'd like to trust you, but I'm nervous.*

A minute later, she received a reply. *I'm a reporter. We keep secrets and don't reveal our sources. I like the picture you have on Facebook. You're an intriguing woman.*

This Cecil guy was on his computer right at that moment, thinking of her, finding her "intriguing"... And he looked so hot. Siena felt the blood rise to her face, as she typed: *Cecil, you sound sweet, but I'm starting to suspect even my best friend of working with the FBI. You'll understand if I take this slow.*

A new email from him—*I think we have a lot in common, Siena. To help us get to know each other, I've attached pictures of me and my daughter. Open them, and you'll see the most beautiful girl.*

Attachments! Wendell had warned her about those. She jabbed the keys writing, *I wanted to believe in you, Cecil, but damn it, now I don't.*

———

Wendell's mind was spinning through all the things he had to do tonight at Sunny State Financial—picking locks, setting all those bombs, making sure the timing device would go off at the right time so no one would be hurt. He'd go earlier tonight and enter before the first security patrol drove by at 1:00 AM, and he'd have to be very cautious.

At 11:00 PM he entered the motel room bathroom. After splashing water on his face, he looked in the mirror, surprised once again to see the dyed gray hair on his head. He combed it back, and attached the fake mustache. "You're a dapper fellow," he said to his reflection, but he didn't feel like laughing.

He drove to an industrial park on the far side of Mobile and, with his plastic gloves in place, hot-wired a truck at a plumbing contractor. On the truck door it said, *Ralph's Rooti Rooter,* and in the pickup bed, there was a big, round contraption for snaking drains.

His stomach felt like it was flipping upside down, as he approached Sunny State Financial, carrying a knapsack full of bombs. He donned the Obama mask and punched in the security code at the entrance. Inside, he put in the alarm code, and then leaned against a wall and tried to calm his nerves. As his eyes adjusted, he held his breath and listened. No sounds.

Holding his flashlight in his teeth, he inserted his automatic pick into the lock on the computer room door and switched it on. The rapid-fire set of clicks went on for several seconds and then a clunk. He turned the knob and entered the ten foot by ten foot closet, with the cabinet housing the computer server. Inside the cabinet he found two banks of computer hard drives—each with three rectangular black boxes arrayed side by side. He attached radio activated fuses to the two large bombs and stuck them under the hard drives.

Doubts and fears swirled in his mind: *What if the computer man is called in tomorrow? What if the meeting's cancelled? What if the security guards enter the building tonight instead of driving by?* Wendell took another deep breath and forced himself to focus.

He removed one of the small bombs from the knapsack. Finding the radio-activated fuse labeled *first explosion,* he attached it to the bomb and inserted the bomb beneath a cluster of cables at the bottom of the cabinet.

Next he took out the timing controller, checking the current time and the time for the first and second explosions: *3:45:00 and 3:45:20 PM.* Fifteen minutes into the Sunny State Financial staff meeting this afternoon, a small explosion in the computer server box would alarm everyone and fill this closet with smoke. If anyone was near the closet, they'd flee to safety before the main explosion. Twenty seconds later, everything would go up.

After installing the timing device, he shut off his flashlight, opened the closet door and peered out. Something had changed. Heartbeat thudding in his chest, he dropped to his knees and crawled across the reception room to the glass door. No spotlight shone. No sound. But there was a car in the lot, and he could see shapes that looked human inside.

Wendell retreated down the hall and entered an office. He peered out the window through slatted blinds. The car sat fifteen feet away, and a distant night light allowed him to see a boy and a girl kissing and caressing in the vehicle. OK to move on.

Sneaking from office to office, he crawled under each desk, opened the computer towers and attached small bombs to the hard drives with antenna wires trailing out the back of each unit. He finished rigging the bombs along the back of the building and snuck into the first office facing the parking lot. Feeling under the desk, he located the computer tower and opened it. Using the flashlight for just an instant, he found the right spot and attached the bomb and antenna by feel.

Light flooded the room. Wendell hunched down, but he was exposed. Clearly, someone had entered the office and flipped the switch on; a security guard or policeman would be looking down at him! He turned his head slowly, but there were no feet, no legs, and the stripes of illumination on the wall told him that the light in the room came in through the blinds. Wendell sat beneath the desk, feeling his pulse rev down. He heard muffled voices from outside and an engine. A car peeled off and drove away—the young lovers were making a hasty exit.

When the office grew dark, he got up, went to the window and watched a small white pickup, with a light dome on the roof, drive around the lot. The truck continued past the building and out to the street.

Wendell allowed himself to smile, as he walked to the CFO's office, picked the lock and planted the computer bomb. With two bombs left, he broke into the CEO's office, installed one bomb inside the computer and attached the last explosive to the bottom of the CEO's fancy swivel chair. "Think about that the next time you plan to swindle someone."

Done. No, wait. He needed to leave his letters to the employees, to set them on top of the computer server cabinet, so they'd be blown all over the closet during the explosions.

But they weren't in the knapsack. His heart sank with the realization; he'd left them in his pickup truck back in that industrial area.

Wendell needed the letters to make this project perfect, but there was a risk. He could play it safe, get his pickup and forget about the letters, but the project just wouldn't be complete....

Heading back to the east side of Mobile, he missed the turn-off for the industrial park, and when he tried to return, the ramps led him into a strange area of plain apartment houses and run-down homes. If he couldn't find his truck tonight, in the morning the plumbing company would miss their rooter truck. The police would discover Wendell's vehicle, and the stolen Florida license plate wouldn't fool them for long.

Wendell would be on the run, not able to go back and explain to Siena… or to protect her from the FBI… or to hold her in his arms.

He was scratching his leg with one hand and steering the truck to the curb with the other. *Stop it. Think. Pay attention.*

Retracing his path, he found his way back onto the highway, to the right exit… to his pickup truck. Now he could head back to his motel and safety. But…

As he pulled the Rooter truck up beside his own, he knew he had to do the right thing; he retrieved the letters and brought them back to complete his night's work.

Chapter 22

As Wendell drove north from Mississippi the next morning, he thought back to that amazing night he'd spent with Siena on his couch, the way he'd pressed his finger tips into her breasts, felt the curve of her abdomen and pelvis, yearned to run his hand down to that secret place.

His penis grew hard against his jeans, and he stroked it, imagining Siena waiting in the cabin doorway with her arms spread wide to take him in for a long, intimate hug. She wouldn't turn away from him when he moved close to kiss her. She would open to him and let his tongue touch hers, and he would feel the beating of her heart against his, and his heart would flood with joy.

What lunacy, imagining a seduction rather than planning a way to be rid of her, but he couldn't control this, didn't want to.

At two that afternoon, he rented a motel room near Memphis with free Internet access. After putting his sheets on the bed and his pillowcases on the pillows, he walked next door to a Convenience Mart and bought three chili dogs and a six pack of Budweiser—his first beers in a long time. He heated the chili dogs in the microwave at the store and took them back to his motel room. After eating the first dog, he hooked up his laptop and hacked into Sunny State Financial's office manager's email.

The emails held no mention of a security breach at the office or of any computer-related problems that would bring a repair man into harm's way.

So I don't have to abort the bombings.

He popped open his first beer, took a sip and then consumed the other two chili dogs. He put the packaging and used napkins back in the bag to be disposed of at some far-away location, just in case the FBI would come here looking for his fingerprints.

At 3:00, he checked the emails again, and then at 3:20. At 3:30 the Sunny State Financial staff would gather for their meeting, and 15 minutes later the small warning bomb would explode in the computer server cabinet, followed by the other blasts.

At 3:45, Wendell piled the pillows on his bed and leaned back against them, sipping from his third bottle of beer and grinning. He would be back at his cabin in a couple of days. Sunny State Financial would be ruined; the truth would come out in the publicity about the bombing. Investors would get back some of their money. For that moment, he felt the elation of a hero... a success, a man who saved others, a man who deserved a woman's love.

Five PM. Wendell finished his sixth beer and walked to the Convenience Mart for another six pack. At 6:30, after finishing two more beers and deciding he'd had enough, he watched the national news on NBC. A man named Brian Williams began by saying, "A bombing in Alabama and speculation—was it the HedgeBomber? Tornados in Arkansas and..." The newsman mentioned other stories, but all Wendell cared about was that bombing.

After hearing the full story and making sure that no one had been injured, he turned off the TV, stripped off his clothes and fell asleep clutching a pillow against his chest, imagining that he held Siena, her naked body pressed against his.

———

Each day, after viewing her Facebook page, Siena checked the day's news on Yahoo, looking for bombings and for any mention of Sunny State Financial. It was only logical after seeing his letters and knowing that the file had gone missing.

On the fifth morning, she fed Heather and Jill the cat, went on the Internet and read:

Financial firm in Alabama sabotaged. Another HedgeBomber strike?

She read through the article, and she knew. "Yes it was Wendell," she said. "The HedgeBomber. He blew up all those computers, and he didn't hurt a soul. And now the Feds will investigate Sunny State, and they'll find out that their investments were crapola." A tingle ran up from between her legs into her core, and her heart beat fast. She couldn't wait for him to get home, so she could take him in her arms.

———

To encourage the FBI's delusion that Wendell had a connection to Omaha, he'd rented a box at the Mail Delivery For U store in Grand Island, Nebraska, two hours west of Omaha. It was a hole-in-the-wall postal store, without surveillance cameras.

At the store Wendell identified himself as Myles Kennedy, and the clerk brought out the package from Blaylock Electronics, sensors for his next project.

But now, all of a sudden, he was thinking about ending his quest... giving up his life's purpose. What would he do then?

The clerk was giving him a funny look—because he'd been so lost in thought or was his fake mustache coming loose? He hustled out of the store.

From there, Wendell drove until he found a deserted park. He replaced his original license plates on the truck and buried the Florida plates, re-dyed his hair dark brown and dropped his fake mustache into a stream. Watching the little wad of hair float away, he decided that he was moving downstream too, bound for home, moving faster with the current. Listening to his own thoughts, Wendell marveled at this poetic image and at the buoyancy of his spirits.

Near Denver, he stopped at a scrap yard and bought a front seat from a wrecked Lincoln Navigator SUV—complete with the seat passenger sensor. At a Babies Are Us, he purchased the most expensive crib in the store.

Six hours after Denver, he pulled into his driveway, parked and jumped out. Removing the crib from the bed of the pickup, he carried it toward the front porch. But he stopped at the sight of a crude wooden sign leaning against the wall, a wide board nailed on a wooden stake with bold letters proclaiming Wendell's last name: "HAWTHORNE."

Chapter 23

The door opened, and he watched her step out onto the porch. She wore one of the embroidered white blouses he'd bought her and blue slacks. The blouse was halfway unbuttoned.

"Wendell, thank God; you're home safe."

He watched the way her breasts jiggled against the fabric as she ran and threw her arms around him. She pressed against him, and his body reacted, but his mind couldn't get over the sign. "What's that for?"

Siena released her hold, backed up a step and eyed the sign. "I needed some things; that's all. You didn't leave Heather and me with enough to eat."

"I don't... You had food delivered here?" The implication terrified him, and he was angry, very angry that this reunion wasn't turning out the way he'd hoped. "You used my name on the sign?"

She winced but only for an instant. Then she smiled. "It wasn't easy. I had to find a company that would send things way out here to Nowheres-Ville, and I had to figure out how to give them directions. I needed a sign of some sort so they could find your dinky driveway."

"And you contacted them how?"

She shook her head and frowned. "You don't have a phone. I had to hook up your computer and use the Internet."

"How could you, Siena? How did you manage? How did you pay for it?" He shouted the words, but she kept looking at him like a child feigning innocence.

"You're not the only one who understands technology, Wendell. I hooked your computer up with your extension cord; of course I had to strip the wires, but you didn't leave me any choice."

He gritted his teeth.

She reached out and took his hand. "I paid with one of your credit cards. I couldn't use mine with the FBI all over me."

He wanted to strangle her, but her brown eyes seemed lovely and brave, her expression trusting and naïve and... and loving... What did it mean, this confidence she showed even as he shouted? She no longer feared him; the thought scared and also touched him. Maybe Siena had come to see the good in him.

He felt frustrated and angry for lots of things, but mostly for letting his eyes be drawn and his fury distracted by the bulging white skin of her breasts that showed in the opening of her blouse.

———

Siena might have been scared, but she knew so much about him now—the way his father's suicide had hurt him, the way he'd written an apology to the woman he injured in that Halloween bombing. Instead, his anger was making her hot, that and the way he kept glancing at her cleavage. She needed him to take her to bed, not only for the orgasms she'd have but to make him want to keep Heather and her, maybe for the rest of their lives.

"Wendell. I've been thinking about you and me and how lucky Heather and I were to find you." She ran a finger down his chest, seeing the way it made him shiver. "But if you're going to get all worked up every time we have a little issue, I don't know."

"Damn it," Wendell said. And she saw that he'd shocked himself. He lowered his voice. "Don't you understand—this is reckless?" He pointed at the sign again, but she didn't look.

"Follow me, Wendell. I'll show you reckless." She turned her back on him and strode into the cabin, hearing the sound of his footsteps on the wood floor behind her.

She crossed to his desk, sat at the computer and opened a page she'd bookmarked on the Internet—an article about the Sunny State bombing. "What's more risky, Wendell, ordering food delivery using your name or planting bombs at some financial company in the middle of the night? And what about a bombing on Halloween by a guy wearing a gorilla suit? A guy who's out of control according to the FBI." She pushed back the chair and faced him. His mouth was open, as if he wanted to defend himself or maybe to protest her snooping, but she had control now, and she wasn't giving it up.

"Don't call me *reckless*, my friend. You're *out of control*, but you know what? I'm glad. You're not the uptight guy you pretend. You're brave and forceful. And I love the gorilla suit. You have passion locked inside, and I can bring it out. But you've got to get over this yelling business."

Wendell, the famous, daring HedgeBomber, just stood there, his eyes wide. She glanced down and saw that he had a hard on. She moved very close, so her boobs were less than an inch from his chest, and then a little closer. And still he didn't make a move.

She was thinking about movies she'd seen, where the hero and heroine shout, and keep getting closer and more and more furious just before they jump each other's bones. "Are you trying to kill people with these bombs, Wendell? Because if you are, you're doing a crappy job. And if you did blow someone up, Wendell, I couldn't accept that."

"Of course I wouldn't…"

"You're building some kind of car bomb thing out in the woods, and I'm afraid that you're going to become a murderer."

"No. It's… it's going to be safe. I don't need to defend myself here. This is my home."

Obviously, Wendell wasn't the strong leading man type, and he wasn't acting pissed off. "Even if you don't kill someone, if you keep on, the FBI will locate this cabin; they'll capture us all. So don't say I'm endangering *you*."

"You stole a baby."

"And you're a nutty bomber." She glanced down; he still had the erection, so what did she have to do to get him to act? She let her boobs touch his chest and her pelvis brush against him. His chest felt solid and lean. He glanced down at her cleavage, and then his blue eyes stared into hers.

She gave him a sexy smile. "I'm very careful," he said. "I'm not going to kill anyone. Let me show you."

"Show me later," she said softly. She didn't move, except to run her tongue over her lips.

Wendell pulled her into his arms. At last. She turned her face up to him. He was gentle and shy. He ran his fingers up her side, touching each of her ribs, as they kissed. She pulled him against her and opened her mouth. They kissed long and deep and sweet and hard, and then Siena led him to the bedroom.

Chapter 24

The explosions in Mobile, Alabama—bombings at a hedge fund company, letters left at the scene denouncing the firm—sent Agent John Motz on a weekend assignment.

When he arrived Saturday morning at Sunny State Financial Securities, a short, blond female approached. She wore a blue polo shirt with *FBI* stenciled in gold letters on the left breast. She smiled, showing uneven teeth. "I'm Ellie, with the Evidence Response Team, and you, I believe are Special Agent Motz."

"I believe that too, Ellie." Motz shook her hand.

"Small bombs took out every personal computer in this company, and larger ones wiped out the computer server. Lots of evidence to keep my team working over the weekend."

"They don't give those snazzy polo shirts to us guys who only work six days a week," he said.

"Yeah." She grinned and gestured for him to follow. "I'll show you one of the offices first."

As he walked with her, noticing the gold lettering, ERT (Evidence Response Team) across the back of her shirt, he thought that this young woman had a pretty tight body, but she was no Natalie Brown. She led him past a room where two technicians, with the same polo shirts, bent over a desk, examining something.

They entered an office, and Ellie gestured to the computer tower under the desk. "We haven't opened this one up yet, but it will be like the others."

Motz knelt and peered at the tower. The unit looked almost normal, except that the sides were bowed out. "Doesn't look like it did much damage."

"None of them look bad from the outside, but the electronics are fried. Even if people had been sitting at their desks, these little bombs wouldn't have injured anyone, but all the employees were in the conference room when this went down."

He's done it again, Motz thought. *Explosions all over this place but no one injured.*

"Of course we'll collect fragments, reconstruct the explosives and identify the suppliers of parts used in the bombs," Ellie said. "Now I'll show you the pièce de résistance."

They stopped outside a little room. The acrid smell of explosives constricted his throat, as Motz peered in at a mangled metal cabinet lying on its side with wires hanging out. A man, wearing another FBI polo shirt, shone a flashlight inside. The room's floor was strewn with glass and bits of electronic rubble—partial circuit cards, bits of wire, bent capacitors. Strewn on top of this mess, Motz saw several sheets of paper.

She pulled on plastic gloves. "We waited for you, Agent Motz, before we examined these." She tip-toed in, knelt and picked up one of the papers. Motz read over her shoulder—typical HedgeBomber propaganda about Sunny State Financial swindling its investors. And there was a name typed on the top. Motz was sure that it would be addressed to one of Sunny State's employees.

The blond took the paper out into the lobby, pulled a spray can of Ninhydrin finger print developer from a duffel bag and held it up to Motz.

"This guy never leaves prints," he said. "If you find anything, you can give me a shot of that stuff."

She laid the paper on a plastic mat on the floor of the reception room and delivered a quick, even spray. A moment later, light purple prints began to develop.

Motz almost gasped. It wasn't possible that the HedgeBomber would have left them.

Ellie held up the can. "Open wide."

"That crap is toxic as hell. You shouldn't even spray it in here."

Ellie set the sheet of paper aside, so the prints could develop, and stepped back into the computer room. She picked up another of the papers, brought it over to the mat and sprayed it for prints. She found them again!

"I'm glad you didn't drink this." She eyed the can in her hand. "I'm going to need it for the rest of these pages. Now come meet Scotty, our bomb guru." She gestured to the guy tweezing objects from the ruined cabinet and putting them into evidence bags.

The skinny thirty-year-old stood, and stepped between shards of glass on the floor. He had dark hair shaved in a buzz cut and a serious frown.

"I'm Motz from the Omaha office."

"Yeah, I heard." Scotty gave Motz a quick glance but didn't meet his eyes.

"Quite a mess here," Motz said. "What have you got?"

The bomb guy wiped his sweaty forehead with the back of a wrist. "The smaller charge went off first, messed up the wiring and dented the cabinet. Second one did the real damage. And there's an electronic module at the back of the cabinet."

"A remote detonator for the explosions?" Motz asked.

"Won't know until we pull it apart back at the lab."

"It's the HedgeBomber, right?" Ellie asked.

"There's something you need to know if you want to keep your handy FBI paycheck," Motz said.

Ellie eyed him, and Motz said, "If the FBI determined that this was the HedgeBomber's work, none of us could say so unless authorized by Washington. So I won't say it was him."

"I get it," Ellie said.

Motz touched the bomb guru's arm. "Scotty, your findings agree with the witness statements—a small blast in here followed a few seconds later by the others. You might be tempted to think that our nutty bomber set off the first charge to scare people away and protect them from the big blow-up."

Scotty nodded. "I heard a TV reporter call this guy the nonviolent bomber."

"Be silent, bomb man," Motz said. "Neither one of you will ever express the opinion that our perpetrator is gentle or peaceful or any kind of shit like that. Not even talking to yourself in the shower, OK?"

The two techs nodded, and Motz said, "If the bomber used a small explosive as a warning, that was risky. People could have come running to see what happened. Now let's get back to work."

All day, the team in blue polo shirts packaged materials for the FBI Bomb Data Center, as Motz informed Ellie of his top priorities for immediate attention.

At 8:30 PM he boarded a flight home to Omaha. Leaning back in his narrow seat on the little prop plane, he wished for two things: first that they served drinks on the little puddle jumper and second that Natalie Brown occupied the seat next to him, beaming that radiant smile into his eyes.

What was he feeling here? What was he thinking, if thinking hadn't deserted him?—that he wanted to fool around with this 23-year-old, beautiful girl-woman? And what were the chances that she would consider such a thing? He was being drawn in by those hazel eyes, pulled on an irrational course into the land of absurdity. Absurd, no doubt, but a damned attractive delusion!

He leaned back in his seat, closed his eyes and remembered the blond secretary he'd seduced the first year he worked at the FBI. That was before he'd married Sarah, and it hadn't meant anything at the time. But it could have threatened his career even back then, and now, as a married man, married to a great woman, in the era of sexual harassment charges, what could it do?

He pictured the way Natalie Brown had stood in his office doorway as he entered the day before, the way her eyes had drawn him. He'd stepped very close, and she'd placed her hand on his arm, and he'd touched her hand. He'd turned away then, but if she'd raised herself up on her tiptoes before he did, he would have kissed her. She was an intriguing woman... no, intoxicating, and what she was doing to him, and potentially to his marriage and his life, was more scary than thrilling.

He had to cool his jets and back away.

It had been a long day, and he dozed off. When he woke, the plane was landing at the Omaha airport. His thoughts turned to Sarah, his steady, loyal and still-sexy wife. Somehow that foolish itch for Natalie

Brown—that very foolish itch—now made Sarah seem even more desirable.

Arriving home, he poured a glass of brandy and sat in a kitchen chair. Sarah, dressed in faded blue pajamas, her blond hair all mussed up, gave him a tired smile as she entered.

She walked around behind him and began massaging his shoulders. "I missed you today."

He reached back and ran a hand down her thigh.

"Before you get frisky, I have something to tell you about *your daughter,* Jennifer," she said.

He stood and took her in his arms. "Can you tell me in the morning?"

She pressed herself against him. "You're already frisky, aren't you?"

He led her up to the bedroom, and, as they made love, he didn't think of Natalie Brown at all.

———

Motz arrived at work at 8:00 AM Monday morning. He entered his office, took off his navy suit jacket and hung it on the coat rack. Before even pouring a cup of coffee, he dialed Bert Fillmore at the Securities and Exchange Commission. "Hey, Fillmore, this is John Motz. I need to bend your ear."

"Sure, Motz; follow-up or new case?"

"See the news about the bombing in Mobile on Friday?" Motz asked.

"The HedgeBomber again, huh? That's what the rabid TV reporters speculate. Why don't you just lock the SOB up?"

"Yeah, Fillmore. The bomber's here in my office. Want to speak with him?" Motz covered the receiver with his hand and said a few words, then uncovered it and spoke to Fillmore again. "The HedgeBomber doesn't want to talk to you, Fillmore, but he asked me to convey what a crappy job the SEC is doing. And given that this nut only targets swindling bastards, I thought you might check out Sunny State Financial Securities when you finish your second latte this morning."

"Right," Fillmore said. "Think it's another Ponzi scheme?"

"Have a good day, Fillmore, and don't bother to thank me."

Motz hung up, leaned his elbows on his desk and propped his chin on his hands. He sat that way for a few minutes, going over the information he needed from the crime scene team in Mobile.

He heard a sound and looked up. Natalie Brown stood in the doorway. "Got a minute?"

He gestured to the chair, and she smoothed her dark green skirt against her thigh, as she settled.

"Here's what I have," she said. "We've computerized the small quantity purchasers of telemetry equipment used in the SEC chairman's bombing. I cross-checked the FBI computer files for graduate school dropouts in electronics and computer science and people defrauded out of their life savings back in the '80s and '90s. So far no luck."

"When I called Saturday from Mobile, I asked you to…"

Natalie Brown's frown stopped Motz in mid sentence. "Have a little faith," she said. "I've checked with police departments around Mobile about the types of crimes you mentioned. One incident in the suburbs stands out; the night of the break in, a plumbing company truck equipped with one of those, you know, one of those rooter things, was borrowed."

"Stolen? A Roto-Rooter truck?"

"Taken and replaced the same night." She glanced at her steno pad and then back to Motz. "It was actually a *Ralph's Rooti Rooter*. I like that name, don't you?"

"I do, Brown."

Natalie Brown gave him one of her great smiles. "There's irony in this too; the plumbing company only knew there'd been a crime because their truck had been parked crooked in the evening. In the morning, it was square between the lines."

Motz chuckled. "Our guy has a sense of humor; a rooter truck would appeal to him. It could also be teenagers out for a little mischief. If it's the bomber, there won't be finger prints or DNA."

"Shall we follow up?"

"Hell yes."

She jotted a note on her pad and waited, still watching with that penetrating gaze.

A movement behind her startled Motz. He felt blood rise to his face, but why?

S.A.C. Hiram Wong strode in. "You're not going to believe this."

As Natalie Brown swiveled toward Wong, Motz saw that she was blushing too.

Wong looked from Motz to Brown and back, grinning. "This is the strangest thing, but it could be the break we need. You know how the evidence response teams investigate, don't you Agent Brown? One man dusts for finger prints, or it could be a woman of course. Two or three others sift through the rubble for fibers and minute evidence. In a bombing case, specialists segregate fragments that could have been part of the explosive device and fill sterilized gas cylinders with air samples from the scene."

Motz considered tossing his pen at Wong, but refrained. "Skip the preamble, boss and tell us what you've got."

Wong ignored him. "Agent Brown, this whole HedgeBomber case is like something out of *Alice in Wonderland.* There were fingerprints this time."

Motz couldn't restrain himself. "Yes, on the letters, but they can't be from the HedgeBomber."

"Do you see what I have to deal with Agent Brown?" Wong spread his hands wide, like a singer on American Idol finishing his number. "The prints tie this case to another active FBI portfolio. They must have taught you all about fingerprint technology at the Academy, Agent Brown."

"Of course they taught her," Motz said. "But what's the other case you're talking about?"

"You'll be traveling again, Agent Motz. And this time take Agent Brown to provide the requisite observational skills. It's a good thing the Colorado Motor Vehicle Department records fingerprints, because the prints from Mobile match the motor vehicle records for Melody Reeves, the crazy who kidnapped a baby from Santa Fe Mercy Hospital two weeks ago."

Chapter 25

Wendell lay in bed next to this unusual, appealing woman, admiring her lovely, innocent face; her eyes closed, breathing soft. The sexual intercourse—they'd done it twice before falling asleep—had been amazing. He wanted to do it again, but he didn't dare wake her, not after all the times she'd gotten up in the night to attend the infant.

He piled his pillows against the headboard and leaned back against them, his mind turning to a familiar worry; the huge chance of capture by the FBI, now that Siena was here. But how about being captured by her? He'd been in her company so briefly, but he felt he knew her better than he'd ever known another person. How about the fact that, when he'd shown her the condoms he'd bought, she'd told him to put them away and never insult her that way again? (And he'd been so dazed with lust that he'd complied.)

He didn't want to get out of this relationship, not now, which meant that he'd gone insane.

As he watched, her eyes opened. She stretched, and the sheet pressed tight against her voluptuous form. He was getting hard again.

She smiled. "Wendell, do you want to take a bath with me?"

He did.

When he'd filled the tub, she entered the bathroom wrapped in the sheet. She whirled around twice, flung the sheet into the corner of the room and faced him naked. He dropped his jockey shorts to the floor, loving the awe-filled way she stared at his erect penis. How could it be that he had the courage to bare himself? How could it happen that he knew how to love a woman the way he had last night? Of course it was instinct, some message carried in his DNA. He took a step toward her, and she raised a hand to stop him. "Not till after the bath." She climbed into the tub and moved forward to let him slide in behind her. "You can wash my breasts," she said. "That'll keep you occupied."

As he lathered her, she said, "Wendell, you're a really nice man."

He pressed his body against her back and caressed her breasts with both hands.

"I'm grateful to God. He saw Heather and me in need, and he brought us here to you."

"I haven't observed God doing much for anyone, Siena."

"He does, Wendell. He revealed Heather's location to me and then He distracted me as I drove so I would have an accident practically right outside your cabin."

Cupping her breast with his left hand he slid the right hand down between her thighs.

She sighed. "And Wendell, look at how marvelous this is. God gave us love and sex. How could you not believe?"

He wanted to explore, not argue, but… "Then what about the greed in men's hearts, Siena. What about people dying in earthquakes?"

He'd been afraid that his words would break the mood, but she reached down and manipulated his hand, pressing his fingers into her. She moved her pelvis up and down, skimming her back against him. "Mmmm. God does everything for a purpose, Wendell. Mmmm. Are you enjoying this as much as I am?"

Wendell couldn't speak for a moment. Despite her voicing the repugnant idea that this "God" had led her to steal another woman's baby, the movement of her slick back against him was about to bring him to a climax. He took both hands off her body and pushed her forward.

She twisted around and glowered at him. "What are you doing?"

"I don't want to waste this arousal. Come to bed." He couldn't believe he'd said the word *arousal*, or that he had the courage to tell a woman he wanted her. And he was ashamed of none of it.

Siena pulled herself to a kneeling position and turned around. Wendell watched her buttocks and thighs and then her stomach and breasts as she wriggled into place.

"Good, Wendell. We'll climb in the sack in a minute, but I want to make a point, because you're important to me now. God has done things to hurt me, and he's done things to hurt you." She watched him, her eyes reflecting a sparkle from the water in the tub. "That doesn't mean that we ignore Him or hate Him."

Wendell bit his tongue to keep from arguing.

She stood and reached for a towel. "We'll talk some more in the other room."

He followed her into the bedroom and climbed under the covers. She was leaning on one elbow watching him. He reached for her, but she caught his hand.

"I know about your father, Wendell, about his suicide."

He felt his stomach turn over.

"I get it," she said. "I was pissed... mad at God too, but you can't blame God for everything."

Wendell began scratching his chin, the nails digging in. "I... I don't. I never believed in a God that paid attention to me, a God that would help."

"Stop, gouging yourself, Wendell. It won't wipe out the hurt, and stop blaming God."

"I told you. I don't think such a thing exists."

She reached over and pulled his hand away from his chin. "Blame your father, then. He didn't have to put his money in some risky fund. He could have put it in the bank like everyone else."

Tears welled in his eyes. "He wanted something better for me. He needed enough to send me through graduate school."

"Easy money, Wendell. Maybe he wanted a miracle. Maybe we all do."

"No, goddamn it." He'd sworn, but he didn't care. Anger had taken him, anger at Siena, at his father and at himself. He pushed her down and straddled her, looking into her face. She hadn't resisted his shove, and now she seemed almost as peaceful as when she'd been asleep, looking up at him. He stayed that way wanting to punch her, wanting to kiss her, wanting to strike his father, wanting to mutilate himself. Finally he rolled onto the bed beside her and laid his head on her chest.

Chapter 26

Agent John Motz ducked his head and maneuvered into a window seat on the FBI plane that his boss, SAC Wong, had commandeered for this trip. He wondered if Natalie Brown would settle in next to him rather than choosing the single seat across the narrow aisle. And if she sat next to him, what would it mean?

It means she's playing a flirtatious game, taking advantage of an older guy with more testosterone than sense, he thought. Was she seeking an edge by turning him on, knowing he was married and not likely to try anything? Or she was just a pretty woman who liked being admired, and he was making too much of this. He felt foolish and a little angry at Natalie Brown, but still he didn't want to end their flirtatious game.

She stood over him for a moment, and then she brushed aside her long black hair, slipped off the jacket of her chocolate pants suit and laid it on the far seat.

As she settled next to him, he felt a soft movement of air against his face and detected the fresh scent of her shampoo.

"Was that an important call you took on your cell phone before we boarded?" Motz asked.

Natalie Brown gave him a bright smile and gazed into his eyes. "Cozy in here, isn't it?"

Motz felt a little embarrassed and a little turned on and... and married and confused, but he wasn't about to flee from her gaze. "You were saying about the call..."

"From the Mobile police; they've canvassed an area around the plumbing yard where that rooter truck was "borrowed" the other night.... Are you comfortable, Motz?" She laid her hand on his arm for a moment.

Without taking his eyes off of hers, he shifted a little further away, so that his shoulders were propped between the plane wall and the seat. "Go on, Brown."

"A woman who lives in a housing tract nearby reported a dark pickup that didn't belong in her neighborhood."

"Just dark, no color or style or…?"

"Just dark. She saw it around midnight before going to bed and again at 2:00 AM when she got up to take a leak. Is that proper FBI terminology?"

"The word is *piss*, Agent Brown." Motz caught a movement from the corner of his vision and glanced forward. The pilot, a thirty-year-old guy in a white shirt with epaulettes, stood in the cabin doorway.

The pilot shot him a thumbs-up. "Take off in 5 minutes."

"Are these phones functional or are they FBI issue?" Motz asked.

"Just a minute; I'll turn the system on." The young man disappeared inside the cockpit and closed the door.

It's just Natalie and me, he thought. *But she can't be interested. And I'm not either; not interested in screwing up my life with Sarah, let alone my career.*

Motz sighed, unclipped the phone from the seat back in front of him and dialed the number in Albuquerque.

———

Another crappy day in David Webster's life, the case of Baby Shirley weighing on his mind. The image of her mother's exhausted, sorrowful eyes haunted him and other pictures from the more distant past—the dead Baby Chelsea being lifted out of that dumpster 22 years before.

Webster's mind had surrendered to the reality; it had been two weeks since the abduction; he'd lost another infant, but his heart wouldn't accept it. If he could only think of a new angle… But he was swamped with other assignments that his boss kept giving him, like yesterday's bank robbery-murder in Albuquerque. Bates was the only agent assigned to the kidnapping full time.

When Bates wasn't babbling about the red pickup he'd supposedly seen heading southbound with a bearded man and young woman, he was yammering about the Facebook games he was playing with Melody Reeves (or more likely someone who pretended to be Reeves).

To keep his hope alive and to get Bates out of his hair, Webster had sent the younger agent to Rotary Clubs and high school assemblies in Alamosa and San Luis Colorado, to show pictures of Melody Reeves. But Bates had returned, and nothing had come of it.

Webster's phone rang and the caller ID said *FBI mobile*. He snapped it up. "Special Agent David Webster."

There was a dull roar in the background; the call probably coming from a car in motion. "Hey, Webster, John Motz here."

Webster found himself feeling cheerful for the first time that week. "John, the last time we met, you were on your way to the Omaha office. What was that, three or four years ago?"

"Five," Motz said. "A long five. They gave me a nice bump in salary to come to middle America, but now I've put in for San Diego. Sarah and I want to move back before I retire. How about you, David; is Albuquerque everything you'd dreamed of?"

Webster felt like the wind was knocked out of him. "You don't want to hear about my life."

"I shouldn't ask about Angela and the kids?"

Webster let out a long, slow breath. "You're not calling to reminisce about the good days in New York, are you Motz?"

"I heard you were leading the Baby Shirley case."

Webster straightened in his chair. "Yeah, you got something for me?"

"You've heard of the HedgeBomber?" Motz asked.

"Are you on that one, Motz? I bet Washington's all over you. But what does that have to do with my baby 'napping?"

"As we speak, I'm flying your way in a flashy FBI jet. If you pick me up at the Albuquerque airport, you'll have a treat in store; I'm bringing the fashionable Agent Natalie Brown with me."

Webster knew that Motz was a joker, but he was serious beneath the façade. If an FBI jet had been authorized, it meant that this was a substantial lead. "You're saying our two cases are related?" Webster asked.

"That's what I'm saying."

"What's your ETA, Motz? I'll be there."

———

Motz clicked the phone into its seatback cradle and turned to Natalie Brown.

"You lied about the FBI jet," she said, looking straight into his eyes again. "Either that or those propellers turning outside the window are a clever ruse."

"Not much of a lie," Motz said. "Webster will see the plane when we arrive. And I told the truth about you."

She smiled a sexy smile, but she was bluffing, pretending to be interested, and Motz was a guy who'd lost a lot of money at cards by calling bluffs.

"You want to kiss me, don't you?" She leaned a little closer.

"That's the furthest thing from my mind," he said.

Natalie Brown had upped the ante, and in this game he was out-matched.

They'd be doing field work soon, and their safety depended on professional detachment. The court case they developed against the bomber would depend on it too.

He rested there for a minute, his stomach turning over, trying to think of some reason to put this off but knowing what he had to do. Without opening his eyes, he said. "You know the way you flirt with me, Brown?"

"No idea what you're talking about, Motz." She patted his thigh for just a second.

"I'm not sure what you're up to." He turned his head to look at her.

She avoided his eyes. "I like you, Motz, that's all. You're funny and kind of..."

"No more, Brown. You've been playing a game with me, but it makes us look unprofessional."

"You seemed to enjoy it."

"I'm your boss, and we're on a case. And if we're observed enjoying each other's company, some defense attorney will use it against us in court."

"It wouldn't be relevant."

"Believe me, Brown. They'd smear us any way possible. Imply that we were too distracted to keep the chain of custody intact or say that you were only backing up my testimony because we were lovers, incredible as that might seem. This isn't your fault, Brown; it's mine. I'm supposed to set an example."

He saw the way her eyes narrowed. "It was fun for a while, too much fun," he said. "It's over. You and I will act like FBI agents pursuing a case, not clowns in the circus of life." She seemed to be on the verge of tears, as Motz slouched in his seat, closed his eyes and tried to sleep. But his mind was too busy, filled with guilt that he might have hurt the young woman's feelings and frustration that he couldn't do what his male nature screamed for him to do.

When he opened his eyes, they were taxiing to a stop near a hanger in Albuquerque. Natalie Brown had moved to the seat across the aisle. She preceded him from the plane, and there beside the hanger he saw David Webster, at least he thought it was Webster. The paunchy, salt-and-pepper haired man who walked towards him had more wrinkles than he should for a guy in his early 50s. And his formerly dark-chocolate coloring seemed to have grown an overlay of gray mold.

Webster extended a hand. "Hey, Motz, what was that about the FBI jet?"

Motz held the Black man's hand, noticing the flabby grip and observing Webster's bloodshot eyes. "It's a stealth model. Ask Agent Brown here."

Webster chuckled, as he shook hands with Natalie Brown. But the smile didn't capture his eyes. "Tell me how our cases are connected," he said.

Motz wanted to get to business too, but he needed to jerk Webster's chain. "No hurry. Show us the sights of Albuquerque on the way to your office."

He expected Webster to come back with something like, "Don't be an ass, Motz; tell me what you've got," but then Webster's smile faded, and he turned and climbed into the driver's seat of a green Ford Explorer.

Natalie Brown shot Motz an angry sideways glance, as she climbed into the rear seat; it made him feel crappy and mean.

Motz took the shotgun seat, thinking about Webster's Baby Shirley case and its resemblance to that kidnapping from so many years ago that had dogged his old comrade. Webster's shoulders slumped as he drove, his eyes dull. *The man isn't sleeping*, Motz thought. *He's back to his pint a night habit.*

At the FBI office, a thin, dark-haired man approached them. He stood about the same height as Natalie Brown, and Motz saw the way his eyes brushed over her body, not once but twice.

"This is Agent Cecil Bates." Webster spit out the words, and Motz wondered what the young agent had done to piss Webster off.

Once they were seated in a conference room, Motz said, "OK, here's the deal. You heard about the bombing in Mobile last Friday? From the bomb debris at the site and the MO, it was definitely the HedgeBomber, which is the case I've been breaking my balls on for the better part of a year."

Webster didn't blink, but Bates shot Natalie Brown an assessing glance.

Motz gestured at Natalie Brown. "Agent Bates is worried about the offense I may have caused you, Agent Brown."

Natalie Brown gave Bates a beguiling smile that sent Motz's stomach into a jealous funk. "We call that 'in-house language,'" she said. "It's the way seasoned FBI agents communicate, and in this case it's Agent Motz's method of assuring us that he has testicles."

Motz was pleased by Natalie Brown's apparent recovery. "She's a quick learner," he said. "On the job only two weeks."

Webster pointed at Motz. "You've been holding me up since the airport. Now tell us how this HedgeBomber thing relates to us."

"Our bomber likes to leave letters behind when he blows a place up. You probably knew that. At Sunny State Financial the letters had Melody Reeves' fingerprints all over them."

Webster's jaw dropped, as he stared at Motz.

Motz filled them in on the HedgeBomber case—all the places they were sure he'd been over the past ten years, details of the profilers' analyses, information about the bombs' increasing sophistication and their belief that the bomber had hacked into his victims' computers. And now the news about the dark pickup truck that had appeared in Mobile near where the bomber may have stolen a truck.

Webster followed with a recitation of what they knew about Melody Reeves and the stolen Baby Shirley. "Her whereabouts have been unknown since then, but she's likely staying with the bearded man in the red pickup."

Bates had been leaning forward, apparently waiting for a chance to jump in. "And her Internet connection," he said. "She goes online using a sophisticated system with a proxy server in the Philippines. I've been sending her emails, building rapport, trying to get her to open an attachment so we can put spyware in her computer."

"Great idea," Natalie Brown said.

The young man laughed and shook his head. "I was really hopeful, sending her pictures of me and my daughter—of course I don't have a daughter—but she won't take the bait." He looked at Natalie Brown again. "But now with this information about the HedgeBomber, it's a new case. We knew that Melody Reeves didn't have the expertise to outwit our tech guys, which meant that the bearded man did, which now means that the HedgeBomber, with all of his computer savvy, is the bearded man..."

Webster held up a hand and glowered at Bates. "We're getting ahead of ourselves."

Bates sat back in his chair, and Motz noticed Natalie Brown watching Bates with sympathetic eyes.

"Bates has exchanged emails with someone purporting to be Melody Reeves," Webster said. "But because of the proxy server—do you know what that even is, Motz? This world is getting too damned sophisticated. Anyway, we haven't been able to locate the computer she's using, and our leads have gone dry."

Three hours into their conference, there was a lull, and Bates leaned forward again. "Are you going to tell them about the red pickup truck I saw heading back to New Mexico?"

Webster snarled and banged the table with the flat of his hand, but Cecil Bates went on to tell his tale.

Chapter 27

Siena woke to Heather's screeching demand for food.

The bed beside her was empty, but that was no surprise; Wendell was such a wound-up dude, he got up before dawn most days. She stretched, climbed out of bed and walked to the new, beautiful crib that her boyfriend had bought for them. Lifting Heather, she kissed the baby's plump little cheek. "There's nothing you can do to upset me today, little one."

As she fed the baby, she sang softly, "Wendell and Siena are sweethearts. Sweet hearts in ev-er-y way. They love their ba-a-by Heather. Um-um-um-um-um-um-um." It wasn't much of a song yet, but she liked the sound of it.

And she loved thinking about him—the way he'd changed so completely since they'd made it together, the way she felt so protected here now that he was back from his so-called "mission." He'd been such a sullen guy at first, scruffy too, with that weird, shaggy beard and unwashed body. And he'd never looked right at her. But now he sent her adoring glances all the time.

She put Heather back in the crib, carried it into the kitchen and whipped up some pancake batter.

Wendell entered and rinsed his hands in the kitchen sink. He was coming in from his bomb-making, she knew. She wished he'd quit that crap and focus on her and Heather. Siena spooned batter onto the griddle. "I've been thinking about this bombing business, Wendell; if they don't believe you're willing to hurt someone, who's going to take you seriously?"

Wendell turned off the tap and grabbed a towel. "I've done some good with these explosions. They've investigated the firms I bombed and shut them down."

"I read about that on the Internet, and I was proud of you." She took a step toward him and laid a hand on his chest. "It's a good start, but..."

"I bombed the Chairman of the Securities and Exchange Commission. They didn't put it in the papers."

"That's so *cool*, Wendell." Whatever the Securities and Exchange Commission was, it sounded important. "I bet you didn't hurt anyone, though. I mean I wouldn't want you to. It would kill me if you injured people, but they aren't..."

"I know. They aren't going to take me seriously. I have a way to convince them."

She was thinking of one of the *Criminal Minds* TV episodes, when the team tracked a sniper. "Really, Wendell, unless you knock this off, they'll hunt you down, throw you in prison and ignore everything you stand for."

He gestured toward the stove. "You'd better turn that down."

Siena glanced at the griddle and saw smoke drifting up. She grabbed a spatula and flipped one of the cakes—totally black. She flicked all four into the sink and turned down the gas. "If I had asked Heather's mother to give her to me, even if I'd threatened to blow her up, I wouldn't have Heather today."

"Don't compare your crime with mine." Wendell looked a little annoyed but mostly thoughtful. "You're partly right, of course. Congressmen only pay attention to people who bribe them." He pointed at the griddle. "Turn that off and come with me."

She followed him outside and back through the woods to the place where she'd found his explosion site and the pretend car a few days before. Now, in addition to the car bumpers secured on the front and back of the wooden rails, there was a large automobile seat mounted on top. Some sort of electronic gadget sat on the ground with wires running up under the seat. Over to the side she saw a box full of clear plastic bags with labels on them.

He stood beside the fake car, the little lines beside his gorgeous eyes standing out, as he squinted in the sunlight. "This explosion will be a hundred times stronger than any of the others. It will rock a parking garage and destroy vehicles."

"I thought you weren't going to hurt anyone." But the idea of such a blast drove her pulse up a notch.

"I'm taking precautions. Here. This is the controller; it shows time to detonation." Wendell pushed a button on the gadget and the display lit up, *20:00 Minutes*. He pushed another button, and the numbers started counting down. When the display passed *19:00*, he said, "The car seat has sensors built into it. Climb in."

Siena stepped up onto the rail and flopped into the seat. Out in the forest she thought she saw something moving, something big... dangerous. Her heartbeat kicked into high gear. But then maybe it had been her imagination, or maybe something very scary lived back there. Anyway Wendell would protect her. She took a deep breath and looked down. The controller had stopped and gone back to *20:00*. "So no one will be sitting in the car, when it explodes," she said. "How about people close by?"

"That's why I have these." He picked up the cardboard box, took out one of the plastic bags and handed it to her.

Inside, she saw a little electronic part shaped like a metal spider.

"It's a transmitting motion detector," he said. "If anyone comes near, this sensor will shut down the explosion. Before I detonate my target, I will have two dozen of these placed around the parking structure and a few under the car bumpers." He pointed to the bumper attached to the back of the rails.

Siena stared at him. "You're the smartest guy I ever met, Wendell." She reached over and patted his cheek. "And you're a good man. But when you take this much care *not* to hurt anyone, it's gotta tell the FBI not to worry."

Wendell took her hand and kissed it. She felt a tingle run down her arm and into her belly.

"They have to know that I can really hurt people if I choose," he said. "Even the most important people. You didn't ask about my target for this bomb."

"Does it matter?"

"When I demolish the Lincoln Navigator belonging to the Chairman of the House Banking Committee, they'll notice. And they won't be able to keep this one out of the papers. My message will get out to the people—the message that the government doesn't protect us. The people won't stand for being cheated any more."

She couldn't imagine that his plan would make any difference, but his Boy Scout sincerity and his thin, muscular body *really* turned her on.

She unbuttoned her blouse, jumped down from the toy car, cocked her head at an angle and gave him her sexiest smile. "You don't have to blow him up today, do you?"

He turned the controller off, took her hand and led her to the cabin.

As Siena peed, she was thinking that her lover would make a false step; he would kill someone, and then he'd really need Forgiveness. It was *so* important for him to find God.

Back in the bedroom, she stripped naked and climbed under the covers. Wendell came in, wearing only his cute checkered boxer shorts, and joined her.

She ran her hand up his thigh, slipped it through the opening in his shorts and stroked his pecker.

"Your bombs may be high-tech, but this is fascinating equipment," she said.

"Uh-hum."

"It gives you lots of pleasure, does it?"

He kissed her hard on the lips, and she savored a warm moistening between her legs.

She felt the pulse inside his penis. "You might call it a miracle, Wendell, the way this little jigger works."

"Not so little anymore." He gave her a sheepish grin.

"Just who do you think invented this?" she said. "God, that's who."

Wendell chuckled. "Are you going to lecture me again? How about this; maybe my penis *is* God. After all God's supposed to be created in our image."

"*No.* We're created in His image. You can joke, but I worry about your soul, Wendell."

She wanted to talk, but he turned on his side and pulled her to him and kissed her deep and long and then he rolled her onto her back and entered and covered her mouth with his. An orgasm took her just that amazingly fast. "Oh that's nice," was all she could murmur. "Oh that's nice."

Late that afternoon, she woke and found him lying beside her, looking up at the ceiling. "I'll make you coffee," she said.

He nodded, and she went off to brew it. When she returned, he was sitting back against the headboard.

He was changing, she realized, becoming comfortable with their lovemaking. And maybe, just maybe, he'd begun to think about *love* itself. She forced herself not to speak of it.

She gave him the mug, and as he sipped, she said, "Do you remember before we were talking about the miracles God performed by creating us. He performs miracles every day, Wendell."

He frowned. "So AIDS and cancer are two tokens of this god's affection?"

She felt a little sick at the way Wendell was dissing God. "I don't understand that exactly; we're not supposed to."

Wendell held the mug near his lips but didn't drink. His eyes narrowed and seemed to turn darker—his brooding look. "If there is a god that interferes with our daily lives, the message is, *I don't care about you people.*"

"Wendell. Please stop. I'm sorry I brought this up."

"This is too much, too hurtful. We created this God thing; not the other way around, not in our image but in our desperate hope to live forever."

Siena jumped up, paced to the window and turned back. "You're upsetting me, Wendell. God is beautiful and kind. Heather and I want you to believe in Him."

He began scratching his leg through the bed sheet. "Your God gave you miscarriages instead of infants."

"But then God told me how to fix things."

Wendell set the mug on the bedside table and shot her a skeptical glance. "You can't tell me you weren't angry about losing those babies. Did you steal the baby to hurt God back?"

"You're mean, Wendell, and I'm not going to listen any more." Siena carried her baby in the crib out to the porch. She set Heather down, sat in the rocking chair and let angry tears flow. After a while she whispered to the baby, "Wendell can be difficult, little girl, but we depend on him so much, and he has a good heart. We just have to convince him to believe in God to make him the perfect daddy, and then we'll teach him how to pray."

———

Wendell had thought of her as a girl, a girl with a bit of baby fat about her body, but now he found Siena as alluring as any Hollywood star.

He couldn't allow her to stay, but it would kill him to send her away. The killing had to do with both body and psyche. He loved her body, every inch of it, felt inspired by the open way she said whatever came into her mind. He most loved the gleam in her brown eyes when she smiled at him after they had intercourse. And so it would destroy him when he had to give her up.

It could also kill him literally, if she left and divulged his whereabouts to the FBI.

There was a way to avoid the latter death. He'd devised it and hated it and knew he had no choice.

He slipped out of bed, retrieved his digital camera and walked outside, around the back of the house, snapping pictures to show to a real estate agent. The cabin's buyer would have to take the place sight unseen, on the basis of the land maps at the county office and these pictures. It meant a lower price, but so be it.

With Siena on the front porch, he avoided that area. He photographed the outside of the shed, entered and took a picture of the yard tools resting in a corner.

Before the place sold, he would bury his surplus bomb-making supplies in the deep woods and create a new identity. He would drive Siena and the baby to California, leave them in a motel with some of the money from the property sale, promising to return in a few days.

By the time she realized he wouldn't come back, he'd have found a place in Vermont or Wisconsin or some other cold place. It didn't matter, as long as it was frigid and numbing. The thought made him sick, as he snapped pictures of the cabin's bedroom and main room, avoiding his computer and surveillance system.

He still had a couple of weeks preparing for the big explosion, the completion of his mission and a trek with her to California; a few weeks to savor.

Chapter 28

Their meeting at the Albuquerque FBI lasted until 5:30, and when it finished, Webster drove Motz and Natalie Brown to the Ramada Inn, where the FBI had booked two rooms. "Park the car, Webster," Motz said. "You and I are going to visit the bar and catch up on old times." Motz turned to Natalie Brown. "That is if Agent Brown can stand being parted from my company."

She pushed strands of black hair off her cheek. "Watching two older guys get shit-faced isn't my idea of a good time."

"Excellent use of the term *shit-faced*, Agent Brown."

After taking the luggage up to their rooms, Motz and Webster took a table in a dark corner of the bar.

Motz ordered a beer and Webster a double scotch.

They sat in silence until the skinny Black waitress, in a red blouse and tight black pants, brought their drinks and a bowl of tortilla chips. "Set us up for another in five minutes," Webster said. The waitress walked away, and Webster gulped half of his Scotch. "I never thought of you as ambitious, Motz. But my boss tells me you've pulled strings to be in charge of our joint case work."

Motz held up his hands in a defensive gesture. "Not me, Webster. That's the work of my SAC, Hiram Wong, the guy who got that nice jet to fly us to Albuquerque."

Webster shook his head and eyed Motz. "I've been directed to provide man power under *your* command."

Motz savored the first sip of his beer. "Wong's a bit soggy in the head. He thinks they'll make him Deputy Director, if he can notch a notorious case like this."

"I don't care one way or the other, but my boss is pissed." Webster took a tortilla chip from the bowl and bit into it. "I just want to find this baby. We'll give you Bates and a couple of office staff if you need them. Take the SOB back to Omaha, if you like."

"You know," Motz said. "You didn't used to be such a sour bastard, Webster. You put Bates down every chance you got this afternoon."

The Black man reached toward the chip bowl but stopped in mid motion. "I don't remember you and me being best friends or confiding in one another a whole lot back in New York."

"But I liked you, Webster. I respected you. And I've always been a guy who tried to help a man in trouble."

Webster downed the rest of his drink. "I'm not in trouble…. I'm in the middle of a divorce and this case sucks. I'll be OK."

"I'm sorry," Motz said. "You and Angela seemed like a nice couple."

The waitress dropped off Webster's second double Scotch. "Yeah, we'd have been OK if I hadn't brought my nightmares home."

Webster had been right; they'd had party times in the old days, but they'd never been confidants. "It's that old case of yours isn't it—the kidnapping twenty years ago?"

"Twenty-two years, that and a few others. You know how it is with the ones that stick in your head."

Motz finished his beer and waved the empty bottle at the waitress. He glanced at Webster. "Some of these victims are going to die, no matter what we do. If you let a lost baby get to you, you can't sleep and then you can't get up and do the job the next day.

"Getting back to business, your Agent Bates may have seen something important, and you've pushed it aside because you don't like the guy."

The waitress arrived with Motz's beer. Webster grabbed it and took a gulp. "Bring him another, Miss and another double scotch." She turned toward the bar, and Webster shook a finger at Motz. "You mean the fucking red pickup truck?"

"Yeah we've got to consider that, especially now that we suspect the HedgeBomber drives one."

"Bates is a jerk."

"You used to mentor young agents," Motz said. "You didn't let your personal life interfere."

Webster sighed. "Right. I was a great agent. Now I'm a 50-year-old broke son of a bitch. Angela got the house with its paid-off mortgage. She and the kids skim half my salary. Bates is a know-nothing who just received a 10% bump for passing probation. He has no skills that I can see, no one to spend the money on but himself, and a whole life ahead. Maybe I am a sour bastard."

"You're not friggin' dead, David. Your life is going to be whatever you make of it."

"Yeah, sure."

"You won't like this, but here's what I'm going to order tomorrow. Bates and Brown will begin a canvas along the Amalia-Cimarron road."

Webster grimaced. "Waste of time."

"They're going to ask the local residents about anyone who has heard an explosion, seen a new woman with a baby, noticed a red pickup truck or red pickup that has recently been painted."

"If you've come here to humiliate me, Angela's taken care of it." Webster stood and wobbled. "Now I'm going to drive my fine FBI-issue vehicle to my shabby-crap apartment."

Motz jumped up and reached for Webster's elbow. "You're not driving, David. There's a second bed in my room, and I hope to hell you don't snore."

Webster didn't put up an argument, and Motz figured that he seldom did anymore.

Chapter 29

Natalie approached the green Ford Explorer and held out her hand. "I'll drive."

"It's my car." Bates dangled the keys in the air just out of reach.

"This is the FBI's car. You probably own some 4-cylinder Honda."

"I've been where we're going, and you haven't." He climbed into the driver's seat and Natalie took the passenger side, noticing the way he glanced at her legs in the snug-fitting black slacks she'd worn.

Bates drove them to Cimarron, and they stopped at the General Store, where Melody Reeves had bought donuts two and a half weeks before. The owner mentioned several locals who drove red pickup trucks, one of whom had shaved off a beard recently. Natalie thought that was pretty exciting, but the store owner didn't know the man's name.

They checked a few other businesses, learning nothing new, and then they turned up the Amalia-Cimarron road. By noon, they'd stopped at a dozen homes and ranches. "Funny," she said as they stepped off the porch of a ranch house and climbed into the Explorer. "I thought we were making progress back at the store, but now…"

"There's a burger joint back in town. My treat." Bates headed them south. "Didn't they warn you back at the Academy how much leg work it takes to solve a case?"

"Only health food for me," she said. "Take me for a nice, cheesy burrito."

He nodded. "While we're eating you can tell me your life story."

By 3:00 PM, they were a third of the way up the Amalia-Cimarron Road, the homes sparse this far from town, and still no new information.

Bates glanced at her, as he drove. "Did you notice that Webster's an SOB. That's FBI talk, right?"

"Not quite," Natalie said.

"I'm not much on swearing in mixed company," Bates said. "Webster hates my guts, and I don't know why."

"Bad judgment," she said.

"Thanks, Brown; you're pretty perceptive."

Bates turned the sedan down a long dirt driveway. "Our SSA, Ramirez, told me Webster's been through an ugly divorce, so I try to overlook his abuse."

To their left, a scattering of pinion pines dotted the dirt hillside. On the right, Natalie saw a garden with a patch of ripening corn. When they stepped onto the porch of the white house, the inner door swung open, and a middle aged woman peered through the screen door. "You lost, folks?"

Bates gave her a mock salute. "We're from the FBI, seeking information, Ma'am." He gave Natalie a little sideways smile that made her want to laugh.

———

As they climbed back into the Explorer, Natalie said, "Time to call in the Feds."

"Who do you think we are?"

"I mean the real ones." She flipped open her phone and dialed. "Motz, we need some help up here."

"I knew you'd be calling me, Brown."

"A woman who drives this road every day says she's seen a red pickup come and go from a narrow dirt drive in the woods. But the last time she saw it, it was black. And one day there was a home-made sign by that drive that said a name, 'Hawthorne.' Next day the sign was gone."

"Could be something," Motz said.

"And that's not all; the woman's husband heard an explosion back in the woods near there, probably more than a gunshot."

"There are hunters all over these forests," Motz said. "Do you know where this place is? I mean *exactly*?"

The way he said *exactly* made her heart beat faster, and she found herself grinning. She gave Bates a thumbs-up.

"The woman says it's three miles up. Bates and I are going to take a drive by."

"Don't be obvious Brown. Go by once, and wait twenty minutes before coming back. Keep your G-man badge in your handbag."

She laughed. "So what then?"

"I'll round up a couple of techs and head up there," Motz said.

"OK, Motz."

"I'll have the office book rooms for us in that little town, what's it called?"

"Cimarron."

"Meet you there in three hours."

Both techs assigned by FBI Albuquerque were female, in their thirties. The short brunette introduced herself as *Bubba*, explaining that she was from the Deep South y'all, and the six foot buxom redhead said that she'd been nicknamed *Lulu* by her pals in the tech squad. Motz refrained from asking why.

Motz laid a map of northern New Mexico on the table. "We're hunting two nut-jobs, and there's a chance they're hiding out in a remote cabin along here." He pointed at a spot on State Highway 204, the Amalia-Cimarron Road. "You've probably heard about them; the female stole a baby from the hospital and the other unknown suspect makes ingenious bombs that destroy hedge fund offices."

"Nice couple," the brunette said.

"We don't have a lot to go on. The place could be empty. Or there might be perfectly normal people in there, but explosions have been reported. I need you smart young ladies to get in close without being detected."

"Where along the road?" the redhead asked.

"Thirty to 35 miles north of Cimarron."

Ten minutes later, the women reappeared with topographic maps and satellite photographs showing the middle section of the Amalia-Cimarron road.

Motz walked the techs to their black SUV and saw that it was packed with surveillance equipment and ready to go. After they drove off, Motz got into the white Crown Victoria. Webster was waiting behind the wheel.

As they pulled out, Motz asked, "Anything you want to say to me?"

Webster shook his head and drove all the way to Cimarron without a word.

Once they'd checked in at the Cimarron Hacienda Motel and RV Park, everyone gathered in Motz's room. The techs spread two-foot by two-foot satellite photos across the beds and stood back.

Bates and Natalie Brown moved in. "What's the scale on these," Bates asked. "And how recent are they?"

"Taken last month. Each covers a square mile," the brunette said.

Natalie Brown bent over the papers. "This would be the house where we met the woman." She pointed at the paper. "See, Bates, here's the vegetable garden."

Bates leaned closer. "Good eye, Agent Brown."

Natalie Brown glanced back at the techs. "These next photos run north along the road?"

"Right," the brunette said.

Bates slid the first photo to the bottom of the bed.

Natalie Brown began lining up the other shots. "So these cover three miles. Here, see the two buildings back in the pine forest, and you can just spot the driveway."

"It's more of a path," Bates said. "Barely wide enough for a vehicle."

"You're sure?" Motz asked.

Natalie Brown nodded, but Bates eyed the photos for another long minute, before saying, "Yes, sir; I remember passing this curve a little further up the road."

Motz gestured to the techs. "OK, technical wizard women. What can you set up around that property tonight?"

The tall redhead—was it Bubba or Lulu?—held up her hand. "Can't tell until we check it out."

The brunette shuffled through a pile of topo maps and pulled one out. "This map covers the area. The terrain isn't very steep."

"You said that this bomber's a computer guy," the redhead said. "The satellite photos show solar panels on the roof. He could be completely off the grid and still have the latest computers and surveillance equipment. We might encounter sensors anywhere from the road back to here." She ran her finger from the roadside to the back of the smaller building.

"Or along the crest of this hill." The brunette gestured to a spot on the topo map that would overlook the cabin.

"You'd better think about booby traps and mines," Bates added.

The brunette nodded. "We'll be careful."

Webster cleared his throat. "You need to place sound monitors in close. If we hear a baby inside, we'll go in."

"So all of a sudden you believe this is the place?" Motz asked.

"No, but I'll pursue any possibility."

"I know you've had a bad experience with this sort of thing," Motz said. "But we will do this deliberately. We've got two suspects and a warrant to monitor this property, not invade the house."

"That baby would make probable cause for entry." Webster gave him a dogged stare.

"There are thousands of babies in New Mexico, all crying their heads off." Motz put his hand on the Black man's shoulder. "You're a good agent, David; you understand. And you know that charging into that cabin, if it's the right place, could get the infant killed."

Motz felt the gaze of the young agents and the tech women on them. This was teaching time for them, but Webster wasn't making it easier.

"I know who's running this," Webster said. "And I didn't mean to say that we'd attack without precautions. But, if that baby's alive, we aren't going to drag this out. In fact, Motz, you should already have a SWAT team up here."

"Bringing in an army would call attention to us, not a good idea at this stage," Motz said. "Bubba and Lulu will set us up with enough information to make some decisions. Won't you, ladies?" The two nodded, and Motz said, "There's no point debating it until then."

Webster gnawed his lower lip. "I'm going to call Albuquerque and tell them we need a team and we need to be ready to go in."

"No you won't, David. You're under my orders."

"Then register my protest." Webster looked like he wanted to take a swing at Motz, but he just turned away.

———

After dark, Motz and Natalie Brown drove the techs up the Amalia-Cimarron Road and dropped them a quarter mile short of the target. The two women wore black. Each toted a back pack full of gear and Motz watched them strap on night vision goggles, before he turned the SUV back toward Cimarron.

A few minutes later, Bates joined them in Motz's room to watch a movie on TV. Motz dozed off during the 11 o'clock News, and Natalie Brown woke him with a hand on his arm. "How could you sleep with Bubba and Lulu in danger out there?" she said. "Anyway, it's 12:30, time to go."

When they picked the techs up, the brunette hopped into the back seat behind Natalie Brown and slid her backpack into the storage area at the rear of the SUV. "Mission accomplished, at least part of it."

The tall redhead climbed in behind Motz, and he turned in his seat so he could see both women. "You were right about this dude," the redhead said. "He has infrared sensors, and cameras, but no booby traps. There's no way he detected our presence."

"Except for our test," the brunette said. "We had to trip one of the motion sensors to find out how it worked."

Natalie Brown eyed the brunette. "How'd you do that?"

The redhead pulled an elastic off the back of her hair and shook her head, spilling hair onto her shoulders. "The motion detectors this guy uses are wireless, so they send a radio signal. We have a device that listens to the signal and tells us what it's transmitting. It could be just an 'I found something' indication, or it could include a picture of what triggered it."

"Right. You're going to like the way we did this." The brunette gestured at her partner. "Lulu came up with the idea. We found a calico cat wandering around the property and lured him. Then Lulu tossed the cat in front of the sensor."

The redhead grinned at Motz. "Surprised the heck out of the little ragamuffin when I flung her."

"The term is scared the *piss* out of her." Natalie Brown gave Motz a sideways glance.

"The cat tripped the motion sensor and I picked up the signal on my monitor. It's the simpler kind of detector, not the one that sends a picture. That tells us a lot about the subject's surveillance system."

Natalie Brown nodded. "You installed microphones?"

The brunette gave her the OK sign. "A couple of cameras too. It's so quiet out there, the mikes will pick up everything, but the cameras don't have a good line of sight to the cabin. We couldn't risk getting too close, and the forest is dense."

"Listen to this, Agent Brown," Motz said. "Lulu and Bubba, if someone were looking at one of your microphones and cameras, what would they see? A tree branch, a rock, a tuft of grass?"

"Pine cones," the brunette answered. "Your technical team came prepared for these woods."

Motz started the SUV's engine and turned back toward Cimarron. "Did you detect any movement inside the place?"

"No. The lights were off, and we had to stay pretty far back."

"Our sensors have low energy transmitters, and we set up a relay near where you picked us up. Once they start moving in that cabin, we'll monitor from our laptops back in the motel room."

Chapter 30

There was an alarm at one of Wendell's detectors in the night, which wasn't unusual. After sunrise he went out to walk the grounds. Examining the area near the sensor, he saw no human footprints among the pine needles, no sign of deer or elk or wildcat. *No need to mention the alarm to Siena,* he thought. *She gets wild-eyed at the drop of a leaf, imagining bears and wolves and other beasts that never set foot in these parts.*

He moved on to the experimentation site, stopping a little ways off to observe his "test car." It might not look like much to someone who didn't know—these wooden rails with car bumpers attached and a front seat from a Lincoln Navigator mounted on top, but this was an essential prototype.

Wendell's testing had been interrupted the day before by Siena's seduction, but he had verified the workings of the passenger sensor. Now to finish testing the hardware.

He activated five of the spider-like radio-telemetric motion sensors and installed them on trees near the test vehicle. For the actual bombing, there would be 20 or 30 sensors, but five would do for this test.

Wendell set the controller at 20 minutes and started it going. A minute later, he walked past one of the gadgets. The clock stopped and reset. Good.

He retrieved the 20-pound box of explosives from the shed. As he carried it, he felt in his bones the power, felt in his heart the fear that if something went wrong he could kill people this time. But he wouldn't allow it. The little gadgets and the controller wouldn't allow it.

Back at the test site, Wendell wired the explosive charges together and installed them in the harness he'd attached under the seat. He connected the wires to the controller, turned it on, reset it to 20 minutes and started the countdown.

He waited behind a nearby tree at a spot from which he could see the controller's digital clock, but where he was out of the sight-lines of the motion sensors. When the countdown reached 15 minutes, he stepped out from behind the tree. The clock stopped and reset to 20 minutes. He turned the equipment off and headed in for breakfast.

———

Siena stood over Wendell, watching him devour his bacon and eggs. He smiled up at her, wiped his hands on a paper towel, slung his arm around her butt and pressed his forehead into her side.

She felt blood pulsing all up and down her body. But he'd been working; his pants were grimy and he hadn't bathed. His avoidance of deodorant was evident. "Want to go for a bath?" she asked.

He stood and kissed her, and she clung to him. "Later," he said. "I'm not done with my morning's work."

They kissed again, and she opened her mouth to him, rubbing her pelvis against his. "You could put it off."

"I won't be long." He cupped her cheek in his hand and looked into her eyes, and she thought that he was about to say *I love you.*

But he turned, and she let him go. He walked to the kitchen door, turned back and said, "You'll hear an explosion. Don't worry; it's just my experiment."

She began cleaning the table, annoyed that he'd refused her invitation to sex in the tub. After washing the dishes, she went into the bedroom to visit their baby.

Heather was awake, and Siena picked her up. She brought the baby's face close, thinking about what she'd read on the Internet. "I've been studying up on you, Heather. Babies like red and black and white. Is that what you like, baby girl?"

Heather gave out a little gurgling noise, and Siena grasped her under her tiny butt and behind her head and raised her high in the air. For an instant the corners of the baby's mouth turned up.

The sight made Siena giddy. Infants weren't supposed to smile this early; that's what the baby experts said on the websites, but they didn't know Heather. "Do it again," Siena lowered the baby to eye level and smiled. The baby brought one of her little arms up to her face and closed one eye.

Siena carried Heather to the kitchen window, opened it and called out, "Wendell, come see. Our baby just smiled and winked at me." He didn't answer and she murmured, "How can he play silly games out in the woods at such an important time?"

Holding Heather against her chest, Siena moved to the kitchen door. Stepping out of the cabin she called, "*Wendell, where are you?*" He was probably way out back, where he'd built his pretend car. And Siena didn't want to yell so loud that she upset Heather, not on a day when she'd made so much progress. So she carried her sweet baby along the path toward him.

———

Wendell turned the unit on and reset the timer. He walked to his vantage point behind the tree and saw the clock begin to count down. He stepped out to the point where one of the motion detectors would *see* him, and it reset to 20 minutes. Now the final countdown was on. He'd be nowhere near when *this* explosion went off.

Staying out of sight of the motion sensors, Wendell retreated far back along the trail into the pines. He settled behind a boulder and waited, anxious to see what damage the explosion would do to the test car. He glanced at his watch—five minutes to go. A sound made him jump, but it was just a squirrel leaping branch to branch in the trees. Two minutes until detonation. He heard a voice—Siena shouting something, "*Wendell, where are you?*" She sounded a distance away but closer than the cabin.

He stood and began to run toward the test site. There was time. He needed to be *seen* by one of the motion sensors to abort the test.

But should he? He slowed to a walk. A minute to go and still time enough. If she died, he could be safe again, able to continue his mission and save more people from greed. One life against the good of mankind… But he wouldn't have her either, and he'd be killing a person. He moved forward, glancing at his watch—45 seconds give or take. *If I save her, what does it mean?* He broke into a run. *Does it mean that I can't bring myself to take a human life… or is it because I love her?*

He ran in a frenzy, inhaling huge gulps. Twenty-five seconds.

Her voice came to him, but he couldn't hear the words over his footsteps, and he couldn't see her.

"*GET AWAY,*" he screamed. "*GET DOWN. IT'S GOING TO…*" He cut around the last tree, his feet sliding out from under him in the dirt. He could see the controller, but not the motion sensors; they wouldn't see him either. He scrambled on all fours toward the test car.

Chapter 31

In the night, Motz went over his plans again and again. In the Unabomber case, the FBI had sent teams to the nearby town. They'd watched the suspect's cabin for weeks. Motz wanted like hell to follow that protocol; to establish the suspect's routine over a number of days, following him to make sure he didn't plant any new bombs, slipping onto his property when he went out to install more monitoring devices and to get a better look.

But, in the Unabomber case, there had only been one nutty hermit in his cabin, no hostage baby, no David Webster ready to turn Rambo at any moment.

In the morning, Motz assembled most of the team in his motel room. He sat on one bed, leaning back against the headboard. Natalie Brown and Bates sat toward the bottom of the other bed, closer together than they needed to, Motz thought. The brunette tech sat cross-legged on the floor, and Webster stood, leaning against the outside door.

"Agent Bates," Motz said. "What's the news from Albuquerque FBI?"

"County land records indicate that the cabin belongs to a man named Wendell Hawthorne," Bates said. "The suspect has no criminal record under that name."

Motz turned to the brunette—he was pretty sure that she was the one called *Bubba*. "Where do we stand with your surveillance?"

"As you requested, another tech unit will be in from Denver. They'll stay at a different hotel here in Cimarron, and they'll be flying a drone over the cabin this afternoon." Bubba pushed her hair away from her face and pointed to her ear from which a wire led under the collar of her denim shirt. "I'm monitoring the feed right now. There was a partially audible conversation a few minutes ago. Lulu's in our room, transcribing as much as she can."

"Any indication of a baby in there?" Webster asked.

"Yes. We heard bawling."

"Did she say the baby's name?" Webster glowered at the tech.

"I don't think so, but I didn't get it all. Lulu will tell us in a few minutes."

Webster turned on Motz.

"I know you want to go capture them, David," Motz said. "It's understandable…"

"I didn't sleep, thinking about it." Webster said. "We may not have probable cause yet, but when Lulu comes back with those transcripts we may. And as soon as we do…"

Motz felt his blood pressure rising. "We aren't going to have this conversation every five minutes. In case I have to remind you, headquarters is all over me on this. The President's involved. They won't take it lightly if we blow the HedgeBomber case by going in too soon. We'll move when I approve it."

Webster turned away from Motz, paced to the far wall and turned back again. "Goddamn it. You should have a SWAT team here."

Motz had to ignore him. He had to learn the bomber's routine and get a few days worth of prowling in, to gather more evidence. Turning to the brunette, he said, "In the meantime, would you get that feed up on a speaker, so we can all listen?"

The brunette took off for her motel room and within 3 minutes returned with the tall redhead and a black speaker box. The redhead plugged it in, and after a while, a young woman's voice filled the room; "Wendell, come see. Our baby just smiled and winked at me." It had to be the suspect in the baby-napping. The woman and baby were fine.

A minute later the woman shouted, "Wendell where are you?" And then, "Wendell, stop hiding. I want to show you what Heather can do."

Webster was right in front of Motz now, glaring. "That's Melody Reeves. *Heather* is the name that crazy woman called her baby on Facebook."

Motz held him back and listened. A man's voice shouted "Get away. Get down; it's going to…" and then all hell broke loose. An explosion and a sound like static and a few clunks.

As Motz slid past Webster and jumped off the bed, he heard Bates say, "Whoa. What was that?"

"One hell of a bomb," Motz said. "Way stronger than any of his others."

The redhead nodded. "Sounds like debris raining down near our microphones."

They'd confirmed the presence of the bomber. Now Motz was so close to his quarry, he feared like hell what might have happened, the responsibility he would bear if the woman or baby had been harmed.

Everyone stood, staring at the speakers.

For an instant Motz thought he heard the woman's voice, but then the speakers went silent.

Bubba, the brunette, began typing on her laptop. A few seconds later, she looked up. "Two microphones have gone out; must have been hit by debris. The other mikes are out front of the cabin, so we'll have trouble hearing them."

"Goddamn it," Webster said. "Well we're going in there now. And we have only the four of us to do it, because you fuckin' screwed this up, Motz."

Motz took a deep breath and a moment to decide. The idea of a thorough Unabomber-type investigation was off the table now, but they had to stay calm. "Listen, Webster. You're right that the baby is the prime concern. But there's every reason to believe she's all right. If she's in danger, of course we'll go in. If not, we keep our guns holstered. We've heard an explosion, so now we can get a warrant. By afternoon, the drones will tell us exactly what blew up. We'll gather evidence tonight for the HedgeBomber case. I'll call Omaha and have a SWAT team with a helicopter here at 07:00 tomorrow."

"Your dicking around is going to get the baby killed, if you haven't already." Webster poked a finger into Motz's chest.

Motz pushed Webster's hand away. "Look, Webster… David. We're going to get as close as we can to observe. We'll protect the…"

"Fuckin observe? Is that what you want to do?" As Webster shouted, little drops of spit landed on Motz's face.

"We'll get in close and find out if the baby's OK. If we have to, we *will* go in sooner. Otherwise, tomorrow we'll set an ambush for this Wendell Hawthorne guy, lure him out of the house, the way they did with the Unabomber, and bring this to a safe ending."

And then very faintly, the sound of a baby crying came over the microphones. The microphones that still worked were out in front of the cabin, so the baby had to be either in the cabin or out back somewhere.

Motz took a deep breath.

Within five minutes, all six members of the FBI team had been outfitted with bullet-proof vests, dull-green shirts and slacks, and ear pieces wired in to the sound feed from the property. As they drove toward the cabin in two groups, Motz heard Melody Reeves' voice in his earpiece and the baby crying. The woman sounded hysterical. "Can't understand a word, can you?" Motz said.

The techs both shook their heads.

The plan was for one group to approach the cabin and shed from the north and the other along the south. Both groups would watch and listen and plant more pinecone microphones to rebuild their surveillance capabilities.

Motz had chosen Webster and Lulu for his group. He would have preferred to accompany Natalie Brown, to mentor her with his wisdom, to see her excitement at her first field operation. Instead he'd left her and Bates with no senior agent; all because Webster needed babysitting.

Motz's group entered the woods a hundred yards north of the driveway. Lulu moved her tall frame gracefully between the pine trees, as she led them straight in and then angled to the right. Webster stalked along behind her, clenching and unclenching his fists, as Motz brought up the rear. Lulu halted. Motz and Webster moved in close, and the redhead whispered. "About fifty feet ahead we'll have to stop. We'll be able to see the side of the shed and a little bit of the back of the cabin. The surveillance camera and motion sensors on the back of the house prevent us going closer," she said. "After I show you the location, I'll return to the SUV and listen to the replay of whatever happened after the explosion. I'll come back and report to you."

After Lulu left, Motz and Webster sat on a bed of pine needles, peering through the trees, able to make out only a small portion of the cabin. Motz heard the baby cry through the earpiece. And then he heard the woman say. "It's all right, Heather. I'm heating your formula right now."

He looked at Webster and mouthed, "Baby's all right."

Webster nodded, and Motz gave him a pat on the shoulder.

Chapter 32

Siena was fifty yards from Wendell's pretend car, carrying Heather, but she still couldn't see it through the forest. *In a few months, Heather will be learning to speak and calling Wendell "dada,"* she thought.

She shouted again, "Wendell, stop hiding. I want to show you what Heather can do."

She heard a shout and stopped. Wendell was screaming; it wasn't like him. "Get away." She remembered him talking about setting off an explosion, but his bombs were so lame. For the baby's sake, though, she headed for a thick pine tree.

She heard him shout again, "Get down. It's going to…" She reached the far side of the pine tree and turned her back toward his bombing area to protect Heather.

———

As he tried to get to his feet, scrambling toward the test-car, Wendell saw something like orange fire, and he seemed to be flying away from it. A cloud of searing, dirty air enveloped him. His eyes stung, and his body burned. He felt his head jerk sideways, as he hit the ground and slid, his ears ringing, ripping pain in his side.

———

Siena dropped to the ground. "*Holy shit fire,*" she gasped.

For long moments, Heather was silent, and then she began to cry. Rocks hailed down on the path where Siena had been walking only a minute before. Siena backed into the tree, pine needles jabbing her back. She held the baby close, hunching over to shield her tiny body. "Wendell," she called. "What are you, crazy?"

Rocks and pebbles kept falling nearby, and then suddenly everything grew still. Her pulse was beating like crazy, as she stood and looked around. She took a cautious step toward the path. And then she was walking fast, and then running toward the bombing site. "Wendell, answer me."

She rounded a curve in the trail, saw that a couple of the pine trees near Wendell's pretend car lay flat on the ground, and the car had disappeared. She saw bits of seat fabric strewn in the trees, spring coils here and there, pieces of the wooden railings which had supported the seat, and there was one of the bumpers wedged under a fallen pine tree. Then she saw a body off to the side, a body wearing his blue checkered shirt.

"Wendell," she screamed. She ran toward him, came close and stopped. He lay on his back, with his head turned away from her, and she saw blood on the left side of his shirt, a wooden dagger that looked like part of a chair leg sticking into his side just below the rib cage. Siena realized that it must have come from the frame of his pretend-car; the blast would have shattered the beam and sent the pieces flying fast and hard.

She knelt, holding the baby against her breast, reached to touch his throat, the way they did on TV. His pulse still beat. She heard him breathing now, and he let out a soft moan. Leaning forward, she saw a jagged, bleeding cut above his eye.

"Oh, God." Sobbing, feeling herself losing control, she laid Heather on the ground and settled beside her. Siena tried to think. The wood dagger seemed to move with his breathing; it was lodged deep in his side. Removing it could cause him to bleed out, a fact she'd learned on *Gray's Anatomy.*

"God help me," she whimpered. She rocked forward and back. "Wendell I should have told you to be careful before you went out. Oh, God. ...But I did tell you not to blow up any more bombs, didn't I?"

"No you didn't." His voice was a rasping whisper, but it was enough to set her heart pounding.

Wendell's eyes were halfway open. He seemed to be struggling to turn his head toward her.

"Don't," she said. "I'll come to you." She scooted around to his other side and bent low to look into his eyes. "You have this horrible piece of wood stuck in your side."

Wendell reached across with his right hand and touched the wooden shaft. "It hurts, Siena. Really hurts bad."

She didn't think it would be safe to move him, but then pictures flooded her mind—Wendell lying out there in the dark, cold creeping into his bones, beasts emerging from the forest—drooling wolves sneaking close, nipping at his ears, and then, emboldened, biting hunks of flesh from his arm...

There were hours before dark. She could make some sort of bed out of branches and use it to slide him to the cabin. But that might take hours, and Wendell was a big, heavy guy, and the wolves would be moving in. "We have to get you to the cabin right away."

"I'll walk."

She didn't think it was possible, but she wanted to believe, wanted it so badly. If he lost consciousness, he'd lie out there and be devoured. "Yes, that's what we'll do. I'll help you. But you have to hold onto the stake so it doesn't come loose. You could bleed to death; do you hear me?"

He nodded.

She wiped tears from her eyes and then reached for his right hand and helped him sit up.

Wendell gasped, and a little yelp escaped his lips. He sat with his head tilted a bit to the left, panting for a minute before nodding again.

Siena stood, leaned her butt way back to counter his weight and helped him stand with a moan and a sigh. She saw the way he gritted his teeth and wavered, about to fall, and she did her best to support his right side. He gripped the stake with his left hand, but still she said, "Hold onto it, Wendell. You can't let go."

She took a step, and he staggered forward, clinging to her. They moved that way—each lurching forward motion followed by a recovery—on and on, stopping to rest and moving again, until they were halfway to the cabin, both gasping. And then Siena heard an awful sound—Heather screaming from a hundred yards back. "Oh, no. Wendell, wait here." She released her hold on him. He tilted to the side, his eyes bulging, and grabbed her arm to keep from falling. She steadied him, and he straightened inch by inch, and then they let go of each other, and he remained upright.

Siena raced back and found the baby. Heather's little hands were making fists. Her mouth opened wide, as she screeched. Siena scooped her up and hugged her. "Don't worry, dearest. I'd never forget *you*." She carried Heather as fast as she could back to Wendell. And there he was, lying on the ground in a fetal position with the stake standing straight up in the air. He panted and wheezed like a tired dog, but his eyes were open. She patted his cheek. "Are you all right?" He nodded.

"I'll be right back," she said, and then she continued toward the cabin with her baby.

———

Heather was sleeping in her crib, and Wendell lay on the bed, his head and shoulders propped on a pile of pillows. It had been a terrific struggle to get him in this position, with him gritting his teeth and groaning and Siena trying to lift and shove him an inch at a time. Then she'd cut off his shirt, disinfected the wounds in his forehead and side, and plastered the area around the stake with gauze and masking tape leaving a foot of wood sticking out.

Now chicken noodle soup bubbled on the stove. She divided it between two mugs and brought them into the bedroom. He looked dreadfully pale but awake, his head still tilted at an angle. She offered one of the mugs. "You need to drink this."

"Don't think I can. Have to get to clinic in Cimarron before they close, before I lose all strength." He nodded at his side, and Siena saw that despite her efforts, blood still trickled from the wound and ran into a red patch on the sheet.

If she could manage to get him out of the cabin and into the pickup, how could she take him to a clinic, where she'd be recognized... and captured? "It's not safe to move you."

Wendell said something then, something about dying if they didn't get to Cimarron, but she couldn't listen, because the wolves were back in her head. She saw them waiting outside the cabin door, ready to attack the weakened man... But the beasts would wait until it was dark, wouldn't they?

"Not safe to stay here." He coughed again and again, holding his side near the stake with his right hand.

"If they capture me, they'll find out what you've been doing," she said. "We can't afford that."

"Leave me near clinic and drive away. They won't find you."

That wasn't true. Sheriffs would investigate when a man was wounded in an explosion, so she'd have to flee from this great setup and take her baby to an uncertain fate somewhere far away. "You're getting too nervous about this, Wendell. I can nurse you to health."

She was thinking she'd keep him still and keep disinfecting the wound. Tonight on the Internet she'd order antibiotics to be delivered here to the cabin. They would leave the stake in place until he started to feel better and then she'd saw it off close to his body; people lived just fine with all sorts of things lodged inside them.

The next time he coughed, the hand he used to cover his mouth came away spattered in blood and mucous. She stared at it for a long time, tears running down her cheeks.

Even if Wendell didn't make it, they could have a good life here. Siena would order all their supplies from the Internet, and she'd teach Heather how to read and go online. Her baby would grow up to be a beautiful, intelligent woman. "We have to pray, so God will cure you. Hold my hand, and we'll pray together."

———

Wendell lay with his eyes closed, feeling the incessant pain in his side, feeling his life bleeding away but not having the strength to get up. If he moved, the ripping agony would return. "Siena."

She didn't answer. How long had she been gone from the room? "Siena." Was he saying her name out loud or only thinking it?

He'd been dreaming about intercourse with her, and then he woke to this pain and the fear that he'd die never having the chance to savor her body again.

The loss of her body and the end of his mission. Without him, the scoundrels of the world could steal everything they wanted, but he didn't care. Let them swindle gullible men like his father. Perhaps Siena had been right; maybe Dad was just another member of the greedy hoard.

When she had held his hand before and prayed for him, he'd felt cared for and comforted, even though he didn't believe. "Siena, I need you," he called. A spasm of coughing shook him and ripped through his side.

Chapter 33

As Motz sat with Webster in the forest near Wendell Hawthorne's shed, they heard the woman's voice—from inside the cabin—several times on the audio feed in their ear buds. And Motz could see Webster relax a little more each time they heard the infant cry.

When Lulu returned, she reported in a whisper. "From our cameras, we got a shot between the trees a few minutes after the explosion. First the woman carried the baby to the cabin. She left and returned with the man. He must have been wounded, because she had her arm around him, helping him onto the back porch. We couldn't see his left side, but he seemed to wince when he stepped with that foot."

"Could be a foot or leg injury," Motz said.

Lulu nodded.

Motz couldn't stop thinking that his chances for a detailed Unabomber-type investigation were now all shot to hell. Still, unless there was a new emergency, he would not give up tonight's reconnaissance. Tomorrow morning, they'd lure the suspect out, and the SWAT team would take the bomber down and storm the cabin.

After a few hours without action, the FBI teams headed back to the Cimarron Hacienda Motel and RV Park. Before entering, Motz called his office from the SUV. As he spoke with Wong, back in Omaha, he could see Webster sitting in the green FBI Explorer a few parking spaces away talking on his cell phone. The Black agent waved his hands and appeared to shout at his cell.

Motz finished up and went into the room where Bubba and Lulu had two laptops set up. Motz, Bates and Natalie Brown moved in close to one computer to watch the video of Wendell Hawthorne approaching the cabin assisted by Melody Reeves. It was a short clip, taken through a narrow space between pine trees. Hawthorne appeared to have a cut on his head, and certainly some other injury, but Melody Reeves blocked their view of the bomber's body. *Yeah, probably a leg injury*, he thought.

They moved to the second laptop where there was a clear, live feed from the drone. The aerial shot showed a clearing in the pine forest with a good-sized bomb crater and lots of debris. "Our boy blew one hell of a hole in the turf back there," Motz said. But Motz and this team would make sure that the bastard never used one of those big-mother bombs where it could do real damage.

Webster entered, slamming the door shut. "FBI Albuquerque has obtained a warrant to enter and search the buildings. I asked for a SWAT squad to be helicoptered here immediately, but my boss, Ramirez, says that's your call." He glared at Motz.

Motz felt his gut turn over, but he leaned against the wall, acting calm. "This is interesting, David; in my conversation with FBI Omaha, I learned that Wendell Hawthorne dropped out of graduate school in 1989, the same year his father lost the family fortune and committed suicide. That gives him motivation for his bombings, don't you think. It's one more piece of the puzzle, and we're going to gather as many pieces as we can."

"The son of a bitch also just set off one hell of an explosion," Webster said. "You don't need more than that."

"You know better."

"Bureaucratic bull shit," Webster said.

"Bull shit we live by. You're pretending you don't understand, but you damned well do. This Wendell Hawthorne, if that's who lives in the cabin, has blown up a bomb, but that doesn't make him the HedgeBomber—not in a court of law. Even if we knew 100% that he was the HedgeBomber, he might build his bombs somewhere else, or some other asshole might make them and give them to Hawthorne. Either way, if we charge in, we might never find the bomb-making supplies, might never link him to anything more than a harmless crank explosion in the woods.

"And on top of that, if it matters to you, Agent Webster, HQ in Washington has instructed that we not make contact with the targets unless there's imminent danger. We're to gather as much information as possible about the bombing suspect tonight and possibly for another day or two. We must obtain Washington's approval before engaging the suspects."

Webster looked at the floor as he said, "Did Washington express any small concern about the infant?"

"The Director and the President are aware of the situation." Motz had already decided that he would declare *imminent danger* in the morning, and they would go in. But he wasn't about to say that. After the whole affair was finished, HQ would be all over Motz's ass, if there was a hint he'd gone with insufficient cause.

Bates cleared his throat, and Motz turned on him. The young agent swallowed and said, "With all respect, Agent Motz."

"It's all right, Bates," Motz said. "I'd like to hear what you think. One of Agent Webster's and my responsibilities is to help you new agents learn and grow."

"If there's any doubt, don't we have to err on the side of saving lives—in this case the baby's?" Bates said.

Motz glanced at Natalie Brown before answering and saw her watching him with earnest, assessing eyes. "The question is: how much doubt is there, how much of a threat to this infant? We have training. We have gut feelings, and we have emotions. Emotions can't rule."

Motz swept a hand toward Bubba, the brunette, who sat near the head of the bed, with an earpiece that was tapped into the feed from outside the cabin. "Have anything new?"

Bubba nodded. "The woman has been singing and talking to the baby."

"That's a good sign." Motz said.

"What about your cameras?" Webster asked.

"The suspects haven't appeared outside," Lulu said. "That's what the cameras show, confirmed by the drone that's been overhead for two hours now."

Bubba chimed in. "I've heard very little from the male since they entered the cabin. He's moaned a few times, which ties in with what we got from the camera. And I've heard his voice, but too indistinct to decipher, except for one time when he said..." She looked down at a pad of paper on her lap. "'Siena, I need you.'"

Webster gave Motz a malevolent smile. "If he's critically injured, you might lose your precious suspect."

Jesus, Motz thought. *I want to question that shithead genius.* He ignored Webster and gestured to Natalie Brown. "You've been uncharacteristically silent, Agent Brown. Care to express an opinion?"

She returned his gaze, her look serious. "You're my boss," she said.

"And you're trying to figure out, if you disagree with me, will I hold it against you. That's prudent, Brown. There are lots of son-of-a-bitching agents who would, and you may get your career tangled up because of it someday. But part of my job is to learn how you think about things and to guide your young mind. I'm telling you that I want your true opinion."

Natalie Brown shook her hair away from her face, and her eyes narrowed. "This HedgeBomber case is terribly important," she said. "I'm thinking that if they haven't harmed that baby yet, they won't tonight. As you pointed out, Motz, we have insufficient evidence, and we seem to have a little time to gather more."

Motz looked Webster in the eye and said, "I have kids, David. I love them, probably as much as you love yours. And at this moment, that stolen baby is like my own. We'll go in if the child's in danger, but for now, we stay focused."

———

By nightfall, Webster seemed to have settled down. Motz decided that for their night reconnaissance, he'd let him lead one of the parties. Motz and his group would investigate the suspect's shed, while Webster's party went over the explosion site.

Around 10:00 Bubba led Motz and Natalie Brown, all three wearing dark clothes and night vision goggles, to the back of Wendell Hawthorne's shed.

As Bubba opened a box cutter and began slicing slivers off one of the wall boards on the shed, Natalie Brown and Motz slipped off their goggles.

She moved close to Motz and whispered, "I was surprised you let Webster out of your sight. Think he'll be OK?"

Motz felt a wisp of her hair blow against his cheek. "It's not just Webster that worries me. I want that baby out of there too. And if the damned bomber dies, all the evidence in the world won't convict a corpse."

Bubba inserted the foot-long probe of a fiber optic scope into the hole she'd cut. After shifting it around for a couple of minutes, she whispered to Motz, "Look."

The tech held the scope for him, and he leaned close to the three-inch-wide monitor. In its green glow he spotted a rack of jars behind a workbench, but he couldn't read the labels on them. "Chemicals," Bubba said. Motz stepped back to let Natalie Brown take a look, and then the tech repositioned the scope and murmured, "This could be some sort of actuator."

Motz gazed at the screen again and saw an electronic box on a shelf inside the shed. It had buttons and a little digital screen, like the controller the bomber had used at Sunny State Financial. He felt himself grinning, as he touched Natalie Brown's arm and pointed at the scope. "I saw one of these before, down in Mobile."

"So this is the evidence we need to make our case?"

"Right, Brown."

"Are we going to break in?" she asked.

"Don't be over-anxious," he said. "That would make noise, and it could trip a booby trap or warning device. Either way it might endanger that sweet, stolen baby. A forensic team will take this place apart after we capture them."

———

Back at the motel they met Webster's team in the room.

"We found the black pile of rubble you asked us to check out, but there won't be much evidence in that bomb crater," Webster said. "Now, where's the damned SWAT team you ordered?"

"SWAT is asleep right now, but they'll be here at 0-700. We'll get up at 0-600 to review any new surveillance. When the team arrives, we'll devise a plan to lure these bastards out and take prisoners."

"You expect me to sit here in this crappy motel a half-hour drive away, while they kill that infant?" Webster's forehead was covered in sweat, and he was clenching and unclenching his fists. "You have what you need, we could go now."

"Take a tranquilizer if you have to, David. You know it's more dangerous at night, and it would be foolhardy to charge in."

Motz glanced at Bubba, Bates and Natalie Brown, all sitting on the bed. Natalie Brown looked worried as hell.

Webster wagged a finger at him. "We can catch them in their sleep. We have night vision equipment."

"We're not SWAT," Motz said. "And this guy has alarms. We have new agents to consider and us older guys who haven't led a raid in a decade. We'll approach in the morning and send someone innocent looking, like Agent Brown here, to lure Hawthorne and the woman outside, take the perps without endangering the infant."

Webster spat on the floor. "That would have been a better approach, if we'd done it this morning."

Motz saw Natalie Brown eyeing them both, as Webster said, "When you and I were drinking the other night, did I mention how we lost that baby 22 years ago?"

"You didn't have to, David."

"We delayed a few minutes too long, while we talked the situation over." The Black agent's eyes grew watery, as he spoke. "The bastards slaughtered that infant and threw her in a goddamned dumpster. I went along with your evidence gathering, Motz, because it had a purpose and HQ demanded it, but I'm not going to let a further delay cause another baby to die."

"My plan is the best to avoid loss of life," Motz said. "Not only the baby's but the suspects' and these agents' as well." He pointed at Bates and Brown, both sitting at the bottom of the bed.

"I don't care." Webster pulled out a handkerchief and wiped his nose. "The man's injured and desperate. You can tell me again that you've been put in charge. Report me to headquarters, and have me demoted. I can't leave that baby unprotected."

"It could mean your pension."

"Tell me about that tomorrow," Webster snarled. "Tonight, I only care about that baby."

"*Wait.*" Natalie Brown stood and stepped toward Webster. "What if we could be close enough to the cabin to charge in, if anything went down?"

Everyone stared at her, as she said, "We can set up in the SUVs nearby and monitor the microphones all night. If necessary, we go in; otherwise we follow Motz's plan. Does that work for you, Agent Webster?"

Webster was shaking his head, looking a little less belligerent.

"We need to be fresh in the morning," Motz said.

Natalie Brown held her palm in front of Motz's face. "I'm trying to negotiate something here, Motz. Tell me your objections, after I finish with *him.*" She nodded at Webster. "Will it work for you, Agent Webster? You can protect the baby *and* keep your pension."

"All right," Webster said.

She eyed Motz. "Bates and I will be fresh in the morning, Agent Motz, because we're *new agents*, and we'll have enough adrenaline running up our asses to keep us awake for a week. OK?"

Motz was thinking that if he didn't want to get a good agent—who happened to be an old friend—fired, he'd better accept Natalie Brown's suggestion. Not only that but he was surprised and damned proud of the young woman. "OK, we'll camp in the SUVs tonight."

Chapter 34

Shadows filled the spaces between the trees out back of the cabin. Siena paced back and forth across the main room, her arms wrapped around her chest. She looked at the bedroom door, longing to wake Wendell, but he needed rest. A scraping sound outside sent her running to the front window. She parted the curtains and peered out. In the corner of her vision, she caught movement, turned her head but saw only trees and blackness. Maybe it had been nothing, but the beasts of the forest could be very sneaky.

She blocked the back door with the armchair and struggled to move the couch against the front door. Thinking back to the vision she'd seen earlier—she was pretty sure it had been her imagination—wolves hadn't really been lapping Wendell's blood from the stake in his side.

As she warmed formula for the baby, she glanced out the kitchen window and caught another movement, but again, when she focused, she saw only forest. Her blood was pumping so hard it pounded in her ears, but her ears seemed to be floating a foot or two above her head.

She shut off the burner under the warming pan and rushed into the bedroom. Her patient was asleep. Beads of sweat covered his forehead, and the pillows were wet by his shoulders and head. Blood still dripped from the wound in his side. And red splotches covered the towel she'd left on his pillow.

She touched his hand. When he didn't move, she grasped it harder and tugged.

He groaned and opened his eyes.

"Wendell, do you feel good enough to sit with me in the living room? I need you to help scare the wolves away."

"Keep the door closed; they won't get in."

Obviously, he wasn't going to be much help. "You've gotta teach me how to use your shotgun."

"No ammunition. I blew it up." His chest heaved with a hacking cough, and his face contorted with pain. He spit into the bloody towel and pulled in a raspy breath. "Trying to hang on 'til morning. Take me to clinic then."

"Wendell, there are wolves and mountain lions out there."

Wendell closed his eyes. "No more talk," he said.

Maybe he was right; maybe she'd be safe if she just stayed close to him. "Wendell you have to pray. God will listen, because in your heart, you're a good man."

He sighed, and she thought he looked peaceful. Sliding into bed beside him, she snuggled close and took his hand, thinking that the stake in his side was wooden, like Christ's crucifix. Wendell was a holy man, only he didn't know it. He was suffering for mankind's sins. "God, you've given me Heather to adore and Wendell to take care of us. You've taken so much, but you mustn't take him."

She heard the baby crying in the other room and realized that it had been going on for a while. Heather had begun to shriek now, but Siena had to stay here and help Wendell talk with God. If Siena and Wendell prayed together, all their problems could be solved. God would even make Heather calm down.

Wendell's face looked peaceful, and she sensed that he was praying too. He spoke to her and to God, silently, but she thought she heard his words.

———

Siena woke with a start. Heather still bawling in the kitchen, and Wendell still held her fingers with his limp hand. "Did you and God have a good conversation?" she asked.

Yes. She heard his clear answer, though his lips didn't move—so Wendell was communicating with his thoughts again. *I'm at peace with the Lord,* he was thinking.

His hand wasn't hot like before. She let go of it and ran her fingers up to his forehead—not sweaty. He was getting better.

And she was still hearing his thoughts. *Lord, God I believe in you now. Heal me, so I can take care of Siena and our baby. Help me prosper, so I can buy Siena the things she needs and teach Heather about computers when she gets older.*

"Wake up, Wendell. I'll make you dinner," she said.

When he didn't answer, she squeezed his hand hard, but he didn't open his eyes. "Why won't you talk with me? You're making me feel really bad. Stop that crying, Heather. You're pissing us off in here."

She jumped off the bed and pulled hard on his hand. His upper body jerked and his head bumped the headboard, but he didn't react. She walked around and looked at the wound in his side; no blood dripping. That was good, but he had to speak to help her feel better. She tried to think of something to encourage him. "Wendell, really soon, when the wolves go away, I'll take you to the clinic, but you have to wake up." Still nothing.

She looked up then and thought she saw one of the wolves peeking out from the bathroom doorway and then slipping out of view. Wendell had slipped away too, hadn't he?

"Oh, God. What have you done?" She screamed and cried and kept on screaming…

Chapter 35

Motz and Webster sat in the bucket seats of the techs' black SUV, parked on a dirt Forest Service road a few hundred yards from the suspects' cabin. The SUV was facing out with engine running. Bubba and Lulu sat in the back seat, and the sound feed from the cabin was wired into the SUV's dashboard speakers.

Motz wasn't getting a whole lot of sleep. He'd never been able to doze sitting up, and then there was the uncomfortable bullet proof vest strapped around his chest. Natalie Brown and Bates were alone together in the green Explorer, which was parked behind them. Motz looked in the rearview mirror, but couldn't make out anything in the darkened vehicle.

"The baby's been crying for almost an hour," Webster said. "Not just crying, wailing."

"That's what babies do," Motz said. But it was making him nervous too. More than several minutes for a newborn infant seemed like too much, and he thought he heard hoarseness in the infant's cry. But crying wasn't life-threatening; charging into a suspect's cabin could be.

"That woman isn't doing anything about it." Webster reached over and turned the volume way up. "Maybe now you can hear the baby's distress, Motz."

Motz lowered it. "For all we know the woman's trying to soothe the baby; it could be colic or something." Motz hated the fact that he'd misjudged how quickly this would come to a head. He should have ordered SWAT a day before as Webster had demanded. Maybe if Webster hadn't been such a pain in the ass, he would have.

"That bitch is neglecting the infant," Webster said.

Motz's boss, Wong, would second guess him either way, and Washington wouldn't be forgiving if this turned out badly. "You have a point, David, but we'll give it more time."

The dull green light from the dashboard illuminated Webster's eyes, as he said, "Will you agree to fifteen minutes? If you don't, I'll be out this door and headed up there right now."

"Stay put, David; crying never killed a baby. If we go, we won't be charging in like assholes. We'll make a careful approach."

He heard the woman's voice coming from the speakers, at first indistinct. He missed part of it but made out the words, *"talk to me."* Too bad that the microphones were outside the cabin. But then she yelled at the baby, "Stop that crying, Heather. You're pissing us off in here." Webster sat straight in his seat and glared. Motz heard the woman shout, "Oh, God. What have you done?" And then she shrieked like a mad woman.

"That did it." Webster opened the door latch on his side of the SUV.

"Stay in the vehicle," Motz ordered. He picked up the microphone to the two way radio.

"Fuck you," Webster said. "I'm going in,"

"Don't be a jerk, Webster. We're *all* going in." Motz keyed the mike. "Brown and Bates, wake up and strap on your weapons."

Chapter 36

S iena stopped screaming and tried to think, but there were too many voices inside her head. Maybe there was a way to rouse Wendell. She climbed back into the bed, pressing her breasts into him. "Come on, dear, wake up." When he didn't move, she sat up again, sobbing. "Please, God, please heal Wendell. He's a good man."

She heard a boom and a crash by the front door and thuds at the back of the cabin too. Sounds that seemed like men's voices, but it had to be wolves; they were very cunning, able to turn into vampires and imitate human speech.

She jumped up and moved to the open door to the main room, planning to run into the kitchen for a knife, but it was too late. They swarmed into the front room, hurling the chair aside and leaping over the couch, dressed as men, wearing navy blue vests that said "FBI" in bold yellow letters …like on TV. One of them darted like a lion to the kitchen, to the crib that held her dear babe.

She had to protect Heather and Wendell too. Balling her hands into fists, she took a step into the main room, but two beasts came at her. One of them, who looked like a large Black man, smacked into her. As the beast wrapped its arms around her and propelled her toward the bed, she felt the flabbiness of his body. She landed on the bed beside her beloved, and the beast pinned her there, holding her wrists in a monstrous grip.

"Wendell," she gasped. "You've got to wake up now."

One of the animals, masquerading as a thin dark-haired man, bent over Wendell and felt for a pulse at his neck. The beast turned his head, and Siena recognized him. He was that nice reporter who'd sent his picture to her on Facebook, the one who wanted to do her story. The wolf was Cecil Bates.

Chapter 37

With the help of the local sheriff, Special Agents David Webster and Cecil Bates rousted the only pediatrician in Cimarron, NM at 5:00 AM. As the doctor examined little Shirley Cavendish, Webster called his boss, SSA Ramirez. After congratulating Webster, Ramirez said, "Once you have medical clearance, bring the baby to Albuquerque for the reunion with her parents."

"We should do it in Santa Fe, less of a trip for the infant."

"Webster, think. The media is here in Albuquerque."

"The Cavendish family lives nearby. We should think of them."

"I'm your boss, and I'm in Albuquerque. Collins is my boss, and he's in Albuquerque. Collins will love getting his mug in front of the cameras." Ramirez sighed. "I don't know why I expect you to think like management."

The doctor declared the infant healthy about the same time that Webster declared defeat.

Bates drove the Crown Victoria in silence, at high speed, rushing to make it in time for the hastily-called 9:00 AM press conference in the upstairs executive conference room at Albuquerque FBI headquarters. Lulu, the red-haired tech and designated diaper-changer on this mission, sat beside Webster in the back seat taking turns holding the baby.

Half way there, Webster checked in by cell phone. Ramirez informed him that everything was coming together; the parents, the press, the mayor of Albuquerque and two state senators would arrive in time. And then Webster took hold of Baby Shirley, feeling more satisfied than he had in years. And with satisfaction came reflection; Webster *had* been a sour bastard lately, as Motz had said. He'd been driven by despair over his divorce and this case. He had ridden Bates and ridiculed the lead that ultimately brought them to Wendell Hawthorne's cabin and from the cabin to this moment with the baby's cheek nestled against Webster's chest.

Baby Shirley squirmed in his arms. Her eyes were shut tight, her lips too. Her pudgy face—pink rather than brown—was as pretty as Webster's own babies had been so many years ago. He wished that Penny and Thomas could be with him to share this moment.

He'd call his children later that afternoon and ask them to watch the evening news. Hopefully, they'd let Angela know. It shouldn't matter anymore, and maybe it made him pitiful, but he still craved his ex-wife's approval. And, in a way, returning this baby to her parents felt like vindication for all the long hours he hadn't spent with family.

Bates pulled into a parking spot by the headquarters building. Webster got out, and the infant began to cry. He hiked the little one up on his shoulder and patted her back. He heard a cough and felt warm liquid on his shoulder. "Here Bates; you take her." He handed the baby to the junior agent and used his handkerchief to dab at the shoulder of his shirt.

Looking awkward, Bates managed to support the infant's head and not drop her, and Webster felt unexpected warmth for the young agent. Lulu looked on, grinning, and then Bates passed the infant to her.

Inside the building, Webster made a beeline for the men's room.

As the two agents stood side by side pissing into the urinals, Webster said, "Bates, you did a good job on this case."

"Yeah, you too, Webster."

"I appreciate that."

"I mean it, Webster. Motz would have twiddled his thumbs all night at that motel while Melody Reeves got wackier by the minute. She could have gone psycho and killed this little one, but you got us into the cabin to do what was right."

Bates moved to the sink and turned on the water, and Webster spoke a little louder. "You gave us the lead, Bates. If I was the one making the speech today, instead of Ramirez doing the talking, I'd point that out."

Lulu met them outside the men's room and gave the baby back to Webster. As they rode the elevator to the top floor, Bates asked, "So what do you think Ramirez will say?"

"He'll find a way to make it sound like he and Collins did all the work, and then to show he's a team player, he'll give the brass in Washington a heaping of false praise."

Lulu and Bates stepped off the elevator ahead of him and headed toward the conference room. One of the legal secretaries, a short Latina, stood near the entrance, and she motioned for them to wait.

"At least you get to hand over Baby Shirley," Bates murmured.

Webster didn't want to let go of the infant. Somehow, the child represented a new life for him, if he could just hold on. But he said, "I'm looking forward to it." He peeked into the room. Toward the back he caught a glimpse of a few TV cameras and a score of reporters. At the near end he saw a lectern with a microphone. SSA Ramirez and SAC Collins stood near it, Collins chatting with the Mayor and a couple of other guys in suits, Ramirez talking with Stan and Rosemary Cavendish. Mrs. Cavendish saw Webster, and her anxious smile filled his heart. She took a step toward Webster, but Ramirez spoke to her. She nodded and stood still. They wanted this reunion to be square in front of the media.

Ramirez came out to them, moved close to Webster and whispered. "We're going to have Collins hand the baby to her mother. He'll be here in a minute."

"Bullshit," Webster muttered.

"It will be good for both our careers," Ramirez said.

Webster turned his back to Ramirez and handed the infant to Bates. "Go now. Take her to Mrs. Cavendish."

A wide grin spread across Bates' face, as he carefully supported the infant's head and strode into the room.

Chapter 38

It had taken Siena weeks to get the beasts out of her head. But now she understood; there had been no wolves at the cabin that night, only Feds looking to lock her and Wendell up. Flipping out had been natural, panicked as she was by her lover's tragic wounding.

It didn't matter now that Siena was locked in this solitary cell with only a small window in its door, didn't matter that the cops and DA and shrinks had questioned her for weeks. It did matter that Wendell had died but not as much as it had at first. The most important thing was the way her tummy bulged, the way the fetus was beginning to move inside her. This would be Wendell's baby, strong and brilliant; not a miscarriage this time.

It had killed her to lose Heather, and she had almost given up on God again. But now she had a glimpse of His heavenly plan—using Heather to introduce her to Wendell and producing new life with him, a divine child from their perfect and erotic union.

The bolt clunked, and a big Swedish-looking guard motioned for her. She left the cubicle and walked with him, passing through the corridor of empty cells, to one of the meeting rooms where her interviews with the FBI, the DAs and shrinks had taken place. Sitting at the metal table, she glanced at the plain, gray walls. The neon tubes overhead radiated harsh light. Two of the tubes flickered, making the room a maddening, pulsing crypt.

The door opened, and her court-appointed attorney, George Horowitz, entered. He was tall, stoop-shouldered and corpulent. He didn't like her; she could tell by the way he pursed his fat lips whenever she spoke. He set his floppy brown satchel on the table and took a seat.

"Ms. Reeves, I've been talking with the Assistant DA again, and I've made huge progress. If you confess your guilt…"

She smiled at the irrelevant asshole. "I've told you, my name is NewHeart, Siena NewHeart."

The lawyer waved the back of a hand toward her. "But in court—I've explained this to you before—you haven't legally changed your name. In court you'll be Melody Reeves."

She didn't like this Jew. He was the opposite of Wendell—fat, ugly and old, slow-moving and stupid, with jowls and graying hair. "Come back and talk to me after you've gotten my name changed," she said.

He laid his hands on the table, giving her his pained expression. "The State of New Mexico isn't paying me to change your name; it's paying me to represent you against kidnapping charges. As I was saying, you can get off with a sentence of fifteen years, if you plead guilty. New Mexico's a tough state, and there's enormous public pressure against you, but for some mysterious reason, they've dropped the demand for life in prison—maybe because of my great charm and my rapport with the DA." He flashed a fat-cheeked smile.

"Your rapport with God, Mr. Horowitz, how is that?"

The attorney focused on Melody. "The psychologists say that you're sane enough to stand trial, Ms. Reeves. It will do you no good to claim that God commanded you to steal an infant."

"Not just an infant, my darling Heather."

"Her name is Shirley."

"As *I've* explained to *you*, Mr. Horowitz, God showed me that Heather was truly mine." Of course Siena now realized that God had intended for her to have Heather only for a few weeks and then to become pregnant and bear Wendell's offspring, but why complicate her story? "I want to tell a jury about it."

Horowitz scolded her with his wagging, fat forefinger. "We've been over that too, Ms.— I'll call you Ms. Newhart, if it makes you happy—you mustn't testify, Ms. Newhart. It would be foolish in the first place, because it would allow the DA to ask some very embarrassing questions. But also it's part of the District Attorney's offer; you will not speak in court, and you will not have access to the press for fifteen years. You must accept this plea."

"I want to tell the jury about God," she said. "Because they need to know, and I'm going to tell them about Wendell, because he was a great man who saved people from swindlers."

Horowitz let out a long, exasperated sigh. "Let me level with you, Ms. Newhart. When I tried to work the insanity defense, it wasn't a ruse. You're crazy by any practical definition, but you're able to understand the charges and follow the court proceeding, so you're not legally insane."

She laughed at him then, because he was too deluded to understand what was crazy and what was sublime reality.

Chapter 39

Agent John Motz strode toward the New Mexico State Court building, shielded from the rabid crowd behind a cordon of Albuquerque police and New Mexico State troopers. He stopped at the top of the courthouse steps and scanned the throng.

Two opposing mobs chanted from either side of a wooden barricade. To the right placards danced above the heads in the crowd: THE STATE MURDERED WENDELL HAWTHORNE, THE BOMBER WAS A HERO, THE HEDGEBOMBER HAD IT RIGHT, BANKS AND BROKERS ARE VILLIANS, TEA PARTY FOREVER.... A healthy contingent of skinhead types stood at the front of this crowd, and Motz knew that two FBI agents were among them.

How crazy is this country, where a nutty bomber reigns as a folk hero all these months after his death? he wondered.

On the left side of the barricade, another horde carried more professionally lettered signs proclaiming, FRY THE BABY STEALER, MELODY REEVES ROT IN HELL and JUSTICE FOR BABY SHIRLEY. They were shouting in unison, "Rot in hell. Rot in hell," as their signs bounced in the air.

Motz chuckled and entered the courthouse. After showing his badge and passing security, he proceeded to a conference room for a pre-trial get-together with two representatives of the DOJ, Washington, DC. The older of the two, who looked like Robin Williams, only in a tailored gray suit and without hair, introduced himself as Justice Department Undersecretary Abel Smith.

The younger Justice Department man, a thin, albino-looking lawyer named Bill Chase, provided Motz with a series of rapid-fire points. "First, despite our efforts to cast the HedgeBomber as an evil psycho, the tabloids love him. Second, the Administration fears copy-cat ter-rorism and demands that we discredit him. Third, no matter what it takes, we will lock up Melody Reeves where she cannot speak about Wendell Hawthorne for a very long time. And finally, we've pressured New Mexico authorities to avoid a trial and put her away fast, by offer-ing a reduced sentence."

"So why am I here?" Motz asked.

"You know the HedgeBomber's murderous plan inside out," Smith said. "And we want to inform the public of every detail."

Motz was getting that old feeling in the pit of his stomach, the one that came when he was expected to skirt the truth for the good of the Bureau. "Murderous?"

The bald Undersecretary nodded. "It's in your report, Agent Motz. He was planning a huge bombing, one that could have wiped out an office building full of people."

"Huge, yes," Motz said. "Office building, no. Try a deserted park-ing garage. Murder's not our theory."

The albino lawyer thumped his palm on the table and pointed at Motz. "He blew himself up with a very big bomb, right?"

Motz nodded.

"And he was going after the Chairman of the House Banking Committee, yes?"

"More accurately his vehicle."

"Forget more accurately." Chase's pallid gray eyes bored into Motz. "He had a whopping bomb, and he was planning to bring down the government."

"So that's the angle you want?" Motz asked. "Ignore the details, and…"

"It would have been like Oklahoma City with hundreds slain," the bald one said.

Motz shook his head. "I have to go back to my original question; why am I here? This is a hearing about the Melody Reeves case, not a press conference about the bombings."

"You're here for backup," the undersecretary said. "In case we need help with the judge. You saw the mob outside the courthouse?

The public wants to rip Melody Reeves' head off and put it on a pole, but there's also a fanatical element of government haters that would worship at a shrine to Wendell Hawthorne. For the national good, we plan to bury this whole damned affair by ending Melody Reeves' trial before it starts."

"So if we introduce you to the judge, you'll mention Oklahoma City," the albino said. "You have the FBI credibility; judges eat it up."

"After Melody Reeves is locked away, we'll ask you to give a series of media briefings about Wendell Hawthorne, the terrorist. The exposure will boost your career no end."

Chase leaned back in his chair and grinned. "There are two ways this can go today. We've pressured New Mexico authorities to reach a deal with the defendant. If she accepts, she'll be locked in a high-security facility. If the nut job refuses, we'll seek a writ remanding her to federal court. She did transport that baby to Colorado, correct?"

"Melody Reeves and Wendell Hawthorne went to San Luis, Colorado," Motz said. "FBI Albuquerque infers that they transported the baby there. Agent Webster from Albuquerque can speak to that."

"Webster's too volatile," Smith said. "Leave out the infer part, when you speak to the judge. Just say she took the infant across state lines."

"Here's the good part, Agent Motz," Bill Chase said. "If we have to bring Melody Reeves under federal jurisdiction, we won't need any FBI testimony. Our psychiatrists will find her incompetent, and she'll be locked in a facility where she won't speak to anyone."

Motz looked down at the table, hating what was going on here more and more. These guys confirmed all the wacko conspiracy theorists' suspicions about government. And now they would be waiting, like vultures, for him to agree to their plan.

But they didn't wait. Motz heard their chairs scrape the floor, as both stood. The bald Undersecretary said, "Time for court." The two DOJ men walked out of the conference room, leaving Motz alone. They hadn't bothered to wait for his assent, because they figured he wouldn't have the balls to go against them.

Chapter 40

Siena stood beside her attorney as the murmur of voices subsided in the courtroom. A door in the back wall opened, and a white haired, red-faced geek in a black robe strode in. She hadn't paid attention to the bailiff's announcement, but the nameplate on the judge's big old desk said *The Honorable Albert Fellows*. He settled in his chair up on high behind that fancy wooden desk, his nose even more elevated, and eyed her.

As everyone sat, Siena glanced back at the gallery, packed with men and women, some holding tablet computers. One kept glancing at her and scribbling. She smiled, as she realized; he was sketching her. The picture would show up on some evening news program.

In the front row, she saw three men in dark gray suits. One she recognized from the night the FBI raided Wendell's cabin—not the Black man from Albuquerque or Cecil Bates; they had both been in to question her over the last few months. This was the white middle-aged bastard from out of state, the one who'd pursued Wendell.

The judge cleared his throat and eyed the prosecutor, "I am informed, Assistant District Attorney Snelling, that the State has offered the defendant a reduced sentence in exchange for a plea."

At the other table, a sharp forty-year-old guy in a navy suit rose and said, "The state can accept fifteen years of imprisonment, if the defendant will plead guilty and concede to some restrictions, your honor."

The judge glowered. "This was a baby kidnapping, Mr. Snelling."

"Yes, your honor, but there are potential mitigating circumstances."

"Do you plan to give her gifts at Christmas while she's in jail, Mr. Snelling, or just one big present when you release her so early?" Judge Fellows turned to Siena's lawyer. "Mr. Horowitz, the District Attorney has led me to believe that we're very close to a settlement here. If I were foolish enough to approve this sentence, would your client accept?"

Horowitz stood. "Your honor, my client rejects the offer."

The judge opened his mouth and then clamped it shut. He eyed Siena. "By all rights, Ms. Reeves, you should be facing life in prison. It seems that someone is trying to help you here. Come up to the witness box, and explain yourself." The guy was giving her a stern look, probably for the benefit of the reporters, and at the same time giving off kind of a phony, fatherly vibe.

Siena marched to the box and sat down.

"Ms. Reeves, has your attorney explained the gravity of the charges?" the judge asked.

She looked the judge straight in the eye. "My name is Siena NewHeart. For the record, my last name is one word, but it's spelled like two, *new* and *heart*. I took that name, when God allowed me to have my dear Heather, the baby they say I kidnapped."

The judge raised a traffic-cop's hand. "I didn't ask if you had aliases. I asked if you understand that you can be charged with Aggravated Felony Kidnapping with Special Circumstances. The great State of New Mexico condemns the stealing of babies from its hospitals. We also reject testimony which slanders our Lord by claiming *Him* as an accomplice in crime."

She felt her face redden, but she knew from watching *Law and Order* not to tell the judge to *Fuck Off.* "God told me what *He* told me."

"Ms. Reeves, did your attorney suggest that you take the plea?"

"He's irrelevant, and part of the crappy deal is that I can only speak to guards for the next 15 years."

"And you decline the offer?" the judge asked.

"I want everyone to know the truth; I have to testify about God and about Wendell."

Judge Fellows looked like he was sucking on his cheek as he eyed the Assistant District Attorney. "Mr. Snelling, is she referring to…"

"To the alleged HedgeBomber, your honor," the prosecutor said. "She was cohabiting with him. But he's not part of this case. The defendant should be banned from speaking about him."

The black-robed prick turned back to Siena. "He's correct, Ms. Reeves; you can't testify about your living arrangements while you were with the baby, only about the alleged kidnapping."

"But your honor," Siena had been rehearsing for this. "When I take the stand, you'll ask me to tell *the truth, the whole truth and nothing but the truth,* won't you?"

"I'll let my clerk do that, Ms. Reeves."

"It wouldn't be the whole truth, unless I spoke about Wendell. He was the kind man who took me in, when I was persecuted by federal agents…"

"Objection." The ADA jumped to his feet.

"And he's the father of the baby I'm carrying." Siena looked down at her belly and then out to the gallery, as a murmur of voices rose.

The judge banged his gavel. "Ms. Reeves, be silent, while the district attorney states his objection. Go ahead, Mr. Snelling."

"Your honor, the people ask for a meeting in chambers, all parties including the Justice Department and FBI." He gestured to the three suits in the front row of the gallery.

Chapter 41

Motz sat in the courtroom with Smith and Chase, the two Justice Department jackals, to his left. Melody Reeves was on the stand speaking with Judge Fellows. She had a feisty spirit, Motz thought, a lively spark in her brown eyes. Jesus, how could he think about a nut-job kidnapper that way?

As she spoke about the bomber, she looked down at her belly and said, "He's the father of the baby I'm carrying."

So she'd shacked up with Hawthorne, Motz thought. *What a mucky gene pool that poor child will inherit.*

Motz had reviewed the HedgeBomber's writings, so he knew what a tortured life Wendell Hawthorne had lived. He'd hated the fact that the bomber had died before they could try the SOB, but he also felt a grudging respect and something close to pity for the bomber. Hawthorne had been a man of scruples in his own bizarre way. And, based on the recordings just before the explosion, it appeared that Hawthorne had charged into danger to save Melody Reeves. Why? Because of his respect for human life? Or had she given him something? Her pregnancy supplied that answer.

Motz was jarred from his thoughts, as the judge summoned them to chambers. He rose and followed the DOJ assholes, on his way to selling out the crazy, pathetic woman who'd given Wendell Hawthorne his only happy moments.

———

Motz watched Judge Fellows lean back in the leather chair behind his desk, a man doing his best to appear casual and in control. There were four wooden armchairs facing the desk. Melody Reeves; her lawyer, Horowitz; ADA Snelling and Abel Smith, the bald guy from Justice, sat in them, leaving Motz standing near Melody Reeves. Bill Chase— the pallid Justice Department lawyer— stood across the room near his bald pal. Motz wished to hell that he had a chair, because his legs felt a little shaky at the prospect of either lying to the judge or pissing off the Department of Justice.

Judge Fellows glowered at Abel Smith. "I received a call from the New Mexico Attorney General last week, informing me that the Justice Department had a *national security interest* in this case. I'm requested to show you gentlemen the courtesy of my court, which I'm eager to do."

Smith cleared his throat and said, "We're here about the testimony Ms. Reeves seems intent upon giving; heaping praise on this HedgeBomber, a murderous felon, who has a following in the lunatic fringe."

"He wasn't murderous."

Melody Reeves' calm voice startled Motz. Motz could see the ivory makeup and rosy blush she'd added to her cheeks. *The glow of an expectant mother,* he almost chuckled at the thought.

Smith continued. "We don't want to encourage other wacko miscreants who might copycat these bombings."

The judge eyed the Assistant District Attorney. "These Washingtonians have twisted the State's Attorney's arm to offer a sweetheart sentence for her silence?"

"Your honor, we can use *diminished capacity,*" ADA Snelling said.

Judge Fellows glowered him to silence. "I'm not one of those bleeding heart judges they told you about at Harvard, Mr. Snelling. The defendant was examined and found legally sane. She was crafty enough to masquerade as a nurse to steal the infant, and she knew enough to flee and hide out." The judge turned on the bald DOJ man. "You gentlemen may control the State's Attorney's office but not my court. What's this national security BS?"

Bill Chase, the albino, took a half step toward the judge's desk. "Testimony that praises the bomber would be dangerous, your honor.

The bomb that killed Wendell Hawthorne was intended for the Chairman of the House Banking Committee."

The judge nodded.

Melody Reeves straightened in her chair. "He wasn't going to hurt the House Banking guy, only his car."

The judge pointed at the defense attorney. "Mr. Horowitz, control your client."

Horowitz put his hand on the baby-stealer's forearm.

Bill Chase leaned forward, laying his hands on the judge's desk. "Listen to the way she defends him. This bomber's disciple would encourage others to emulate his killing spree."

Motz couldn't believe the bullshit, but he did his best to keep a poker-face.

The judge waved the Justice Department Attorney away from his desk. He turned on Motz. "Special Agent Motz, is it your opinion that this HedgeBomber person intended to kill the Chairman of the House Banking Committee or any other party?"

Motz's stomach turned sour. This was the moment when he was expected to bring up the Oklahoma City bombing. He saw the albino pain-in-the-ass shooting him a condescending nod. The bastard's arrogance pissed him off, and the national urgency of lying to this judge escaped him. "I can verify that the bomb was prepared for an attack involving the Chairman, that Wendell Hawthorne was the maker of that bomb and that it would have caused a powerful explosion."

Judge Fellows raised his white eyebrows, his blue eyes trained on Motz. "So these gentlemen from Washington gave you a script... But this is my court, and I'm asking you to ad lib and maybe throw in a dash of truth."

Motz glanced at Melody Reeves. She had a defiant look, as she murmured, "Go ahead, FBI man."

"Do you remember my question, Agent Motz?" the judge asked.

He swallowed and said, "Wendell Hawthorne's practice explosion involved motion sensors to halt the detonation if anyone approached, or sat in, the vehicle. The bomber's prior history, and the diagrams he made, indicate that these safeguards would have been employed in the attack on the Chairman's vehicle."

The judge blew out a long breath and scrutinized Motz. "He never intended to hurt anyone?"

Motz wished he'd taken a Xanax before coming here. He shook his head.

"Is there evidence that Melody Reeves plans to carry on his work, or are these men from Washington blowing smoke up my honorable behind about that too?"

Motz ruled out a response which implied that the DOJ guys were assholes themselves. "No evidence, your honor."

Chase lurched forward and tapped the judge's desk. When the judge eyed him, Chase said, "Agent Motz is omitting the most incriminating fact; Ms. Reeves' fingerprints were found in the rubble of the last hedge fund bombing."

"Away from my desk." Judge Fellows glared at the DOJ attorney, who backed away. Then the judge pouched his cheek and nodded to Motz.

"Ms. Reeves is an *inquisitive* person, for want of a better description," Motz said. "Her fingerprints were found on the letters the bomber left for his victims, but those letters had been stored in the bomber's desk. Her prints appeared on every document in that desk, on the pencils, the computer disks, the printer, even on the back of the computer tower and every book in the bomber's bookcase. The defendant admits touching the letters, but maintains that she was unaware of their meaning at the time. We have no evidence to refute her statement."

Melody Reeves beamed up at Motz, but making the crazy lady happy really wasn't on his to-do list.

Judge Fellows glared at Abel Smith. "You federal crap-heads thought you had an FBI dupe who would support your lies." Smith opened his mouth to speak, but the judge wagged a finger at him. "Don't try to deny it, Undersecretary Smith. And don't insult me with more crap about national security. This defendant deserves no compassion, but she has a right to a trial."

The judge turned to study Melody Reeves and paused before speaking. "What is it you want to say in court about Wendell Hawthorne?"

Abel Smith gestured for the judge's attention. "One moment, judge if I may."

Fellows looked like he wanted to spit, as the bald Justice Department man said, "We believe, and the FBI will confirm this." He glowered at Motz. "Melody Reeves transported the kidnapped infant to San Luis, Colorado before returning to New Mexico." Smith pulled a folded brief from the inside pocket of his suit jacket and set it on the desk. "The Justice Department seeks remand of the defendant to federal jurisdiction for charges of Kidnapping and Unlawful Transport of a Minor."

The judge sat back in his chair, scowling.

Motz felt his blood pressure rising. He hated to be the one who confirmed anything the DOJ bastards said. And he knew what the judge didn't know; if the federal government got their hands on Melody Reeves she'd end up in a psychiatric facility for the rest of her life. That might be a reasonable ending for her, but only if it was done according to law. And so, when the judge turned to him, he said, "We've established that Melody Reeves traveled to Colorado with Wendell Hawthorne, so they may have transported the infant there too."

Motz saw Bill Chase standing rigid, clenching and unclenching his fists.

The judge scrutinized Motz. "*Likely*, wouldn't you say?"

"Yes, your honor."

"But you dislike these men from Washington, Agent Motz. I can't blame you." The judge turned to the Undersecretary. "Submit your writ to federal court, Mr. Smith; I'm confident they'll consider it. But I've asked the defendant a question. Ms. Reeves, what do you wish to say about the alleged HedgeBomber in my court?"

Melody Reeves set her hands on her thighs and smiled at the judge. "I would say that Wendell was the most gentle and noble man I ever met. He only sent bombs to evil people and to worthless bureaucrats, and he tried very hard not to hurt anyone."

Motz saw the tension in the young woman's jaw, watched her swallow before going on. "These men hate Wendell because he made fools of them, but I want the world to know that Wendell Hawthorne loved little Heather. God lent that baby to me, and He brought us to Wendell's cabin. Wendell used to change Heather's diapers, and he bought her things like her first crib. He believed in God at the end too. He didn't used to, but I showed him how to pray, and that last day, after he was hurt, we prayed together. And Wendell said he loved me very much."

The judge eyed Melody Reeves with an expression that was part skeptical and part pitying, but Motz figured the pity was pure acting. Across the room, he saw the Justice Department lawyer whisper to the New Mexico ADA.

The ADA cleared his throat and said, "This is not relevant, your honor."

"Mr. Snelling," the judge said. "I despise what this defendant has done, but it's clear she has other priorities than we so-called sensible people do. I have other priorities too. I'd like to settle this case expeditiously and maintain my court's dignity. I won't consider fifteen years; nor will I cede the case to federal jurisdiction."

Motz was deciding that *the dignity of this court* had a lot to do with winning the judge's next election, which apparently required a tough sentence issued by his State of New Mexico court.

"Ms. Reeves," the judge said. "If I give you twenty minutes to state your misguided theories about God and Mr. Hawthorne from the stand, might you confess that you took the baby and accept twenty-five years in prison?"

Horowitz cleared his throat, and when the judge looked his way he said, "The State's offer was fifteen."

"Mine is twenty-five," the judge said. "This was a heinous crime, and this court is not kindergarten."

Motz was thinking that twenty-five was a gift. By increasing it from fifteen, the judge might claim he was tough on crime.

Horowitz whispered something in Reeves' ear.

"I'd think about it." Melody Reeves said. "But you'd have to…"

"What is it?" the judge demanded.

Every muscle in Melody Reeves' body seemed to strain, like she was holding her nerves in with tight rubber bands. "This isn't really a favor. I'm sure you plan to do this anyway, but you have to promise that I can keep my baby when he's born."

Horowitz stared at his client, open-mouthed.

Judge Fellows narrowed his eyes and looked from her to the bald Justice Department lackey and back. "You aren't serious?"

Siena gave the judge a hopeful look. "There are lots of women in prison with their babies. I could be one of them."

The judge stood and walked around, settling his backside against his desk. Perched there in front of Melody Reeves, he scrutinized her. "It would be wrong to raise a baby in prison, don't you think?"

He spoke gently, but Motz recognized fake sympathy when he saw it.

Melody Reeves frowned and shook her head like she didn't understand. "No, your honor; the thing that would be wrong is to separate us."

"It's just not done, Ms. Reeves. Children need a happy place to grow up, don't you see?"

Melody Reeves shook her head, as tears streamed down her cheeks.

The judge touched her chin, and she looked up at him. "Don't you want the best for this child?"

"I do, but you can't..." Reeves leaned forward and buried her face in her hands, sobbing.

The judge patted the top of her head, but now that the defendant wasn't watching, his expression hovered somewhere between boredom and annoyance. "You'll get to hold the baby, and then we'll make sure that they find a nice home for him or her with loving parents."

Glancing up at the judge, she said, "You seem like a nice man. Why not give me a pardon?"

Judge Fellows shook his head. "I can't give pardons, only impose sentences, and I'm accountable to the people for those sentences. You will have to go to prison for a long time. The best I can do is to allow you to see the baby in the prison hospital for a few days after it's born."

Melody Reeves gave Motz a beseeching look.

"Sorry," Motz said. "The judge is telling the truth."

She began sobbing again and kept on for a couple of minutes, occasionally glancing up at the judge and looking down again, as everyone watched. Then she murmured, "You promise, judge? Will you give me a month with my baby?" She looked steadily at Fellows, even as she wiped tears away, first with one hand and then the other.

The judge nodded. "I promise you a week with the infant, and you can address the media today about your beliefs, but you'll have to accept the sentence."

Reeves seemed calm now, her eyes clear. "If you want that, you'll need to do something for me. I want TV cameras in court when I speak, and I want to name my baby Bobby if it's a boy—which I think it's going to be, because I want him to be like Wendell—Chloe if it's a girl, and his last name will be Hawthorne. Can you promise me that?"

The judge let out a long exasperated breath. "If you declare that the child is Wendell Hawthorne's offspring, the birth certificate can bear one of those names. But when the baby's adopted, it will assume the name of the new parents... If you want to speak on television, you must accept a sentence of *thirty* years, and you'll have no access to the press after today. Have we dickered enough now? Do you agree?"

Melody Reeves looked at Judge Fellows for a full minute and then nodded.

Judge Fellows smiled at the bald Undersecretary. "Ms. Reeves, we are going to infuriate these Washington men who came here to subvert justice in the State of New Mexico, and frankly that pleases me. I will grant you your right to speak but at the same time limit that right to this one occasion. You Washingtonians may leave now, you too, Mr. Snelling. Not you, Agent Motz."

The New Mexico ADA and the Justice Department men left, and Motz took the chair formerly occupied by the bald government man.

The judge eyed him. "You didn't do your career any good by crossing those serpents."

"I got that," Motz said.

"Standing up for truth and freedom?" Fellows asked. "Or is there something else you want to tell me?"

Motz wasn't crazy enough to reveal the government's plan to have Melody Reeves declared insane. And he would deny to the end that he felt a touch of compassion for the defendant. She was delusional and manipulative and guilty of a heinous crime, but somehow she had charmed Wendell Hawthorne and made his last days happier. Of course, Hawthorne had been as pathetic as she was, but didn't all humans have neediness lodged somewhere deep inside. "The truth and freedom concept works for me."

The judge gave him a paternal smile. "It was a brave and decent thing you did."

"It was, wasn't it?" Melody Reeves sat forward and gazed at Motz. "Like something my Wendell might do."

A dubious compliment, Motz thought. *When I get home to Omaha and I tell Sarah about this meeting, and she's furious that I've hurt my career, there's no way in hell I'll mention this crazy woman's appreciation.*

Chapter 42

Siena sat in her chair in the judge's chambers, practicing the words she wanted to say about Wendell and God and dear little Heather, feeling the tears running down her cheeks, feeling that she was about to do the most important thing she'd ever done, telling all of the reporters and the people of America her sacred, special story.

And this was a rehearsal, too, for the talk she would give to little Bobby when he was born; she had to cram everything she wanted to tell him into a week... or maybe, maybe she could dress up as a nurse, like she had that other time, escape with him from the prison hospital. They'd live in a cabin in the forest, and she'd raise Bobby to be a good and worthy man like his dad. Yes, that sounded good.

"It's time, Ms. Reeves," the judge said.

Her fat attorney took her arm and helped her up, looking very tired and lonely. "It's OK, Mr. Horowitz," she said. "I'll be fine."

A guy in a sheriff's uniform led her into the courtroom and showed her to the witness box. She saw the Justice Department shitheads sitting back in their places, but the nice FBI guy stood at the back of the room.

The bailiff announced the judge. A door opened, and Judge Fellows entered and sat behind his bench.

A TV camera had been set up, and lights shone on Siena. A technician nodded to the judge, who pounded his gavel and said, "After some discussion, we have an agreement between this court, the State and the defendant. The State proposed leniency, believing that the defendant suffers from diminished awareness of reality. Considering that position, this court nonetheless found a 15-year sentence unconscionable."

She felt the judge looking at her, but Siena kept her eyes on the TV camera, concentrating on what she had to say.

Judge Fellows continued, but she was only half listening, waiting for her cue. "The defendant committed a loathsome crime and deserves no sympathy. This court hereby doubles the sentence to thirty years without possibility of parole. The defendant has indicated acceptance of the offer, on condition that she be allowed to speak to the press. Is that correct, Mr. Horowitz?"

She glanced at Horowitz, as he stood and said, "It is."

"Mr. Snelling?"

The DA looked like he was chewing on his cheek, as he stood. "Yes, your honor."

She looked back at the TV camera, as Judge Fellows said, "We've arranged a live feed to every television network that's covering this hearing. Ms. Reeves, who prefers to be called Ms. NewHeart, will now make her statement. Before she does, let me emphasize that this court finds Ms. Reeves, her crime and her excuses for that crime reprehensible."

Siena smiled into the camera, wanting to appear as sweet and innocent as Wendell would want her to be at this moment. "When I first met Wendell, he seemed really, really shy. He was a virgin, but I don't think he would have used that word. 'Virgin' would have been too daring for my Wendell. I had an accident; my car ran into the woods near his cabin, but it turned out not to be an accident; it was God's plan for me to meet him...."

About the Author

E dward D. Webster is the author of an eclectic collection of books and a number of articles appearing in such diverse publications as the Boston Globe and Your Cat Magazine. Ed admits to a fascination with unique, quirky and bizarre human behavior, and he doesn't exempt himself from the mix. His acclaimed memoir, A Year of Sundays (Taking the Plunge and our Cat to Explore Europe) shares the eccentric tale of his yearlong adventure in Europe with his spirited blind wife and headstrong, deaf sixteen year old cat.

In his historical novel, Soul of Toledo (due for publication in 2015), about Spain in the 1440s, the diabolical nature of mankind stands out as madmen take over the City of Toledo and torture suspected Jews 30 years before the Spanish Inquisition.

Webster also likes to tinker with fictional characters, putting strange people together to see what they'll do with/to each other. In his latest novel, The Gentle Bomber's Melody, a nutty woman, bearing a stolen baby, lands on the doorstep of a fugitive bomber hiding from the FBI. The result: irresistible insanity.

From the happily unusual of A Year of Sundays to the cruelly perverse in Soul of Toledo, Edward D. Webster shines a light on offbeat aspects of human nature. Webster lives in Southern California with his divine wife and two amazing cats.

See Ed's website, www.edwardwebster.com for more information.

www.ingramcontent.com/pod-product-compliance
Lightning Source LLC
Chambersburg PA
CBHW072231170626
46813CB00003B/1178